Presented to

First Brethren Church

In Memory of

Mrs. Amos (Maude) Miller

by

Fran Wegmiller

NO RING
ON HER FINGER

NO RING
ON HER FINGER

by

Mildred Woodford

1932

MOODY PRESS

Chicago

Printed in the United States of America

To my beloved grandmother,
Mildred Pursley Powell,
who gave a wonderful heritage
of faith, courage, integrity and love
to her family
and others whose lives she touched.

Contents

1

The Phone Call

MERRY WASN'T THINKING of the soft blue velvet party dress in its package on the seat beside her as she swung her little sports car into the driveway of her father's home. She braked the car and left the key so Murphy could put it away for her.

She was sure at last she would not be returning to school after the holidays. Tomorrow she would write a long, long letter to Mike and tell him so they could arrange their lives as they liked. She closed her eyes a moment to imagine what his face would be like when he read that. His eyes, black as midnight, would sparkle; his face would break into a grin that would light the barracks. She could almost hear his shout of joy. Or had Mike grown serious and reserved in the weeks since she had seen him? Not Mike. He would be forever gay, young and impetuous.

Beautiful chimes from the nearby cathedral began to play as Merry hurried up the cold stone steps. She knew the pattern of things inside. Her father would be finishing a cocktail before going up to change for dinner. He would be in a hurry and a bit impatient, as if he expected someone to fail to have everything ready for the evening, this first of the Christmas parties. The Johnson ball was traditionally the opening of the holiday season.

9

Some fifty guests would drift in around eight for dinner; other guests would arrive closer to nine-thirty. Merry remembered the high excitement of the previous year when, for the first time, she had danced even the last dance.

Her mother was resting after a facial, a leisurely bath, and most of the afternoon spent preparing to be the most glamorous hostess in town. Her mother always followed the same ritual the day of the Christmas ball or any other large party. Druscilla Johnson rarely left her room at such times until she was ready to descend the stairs, radiant in a fabulous dress and glittering jewels, her hair perfect from the fingers of Madame Marie.

Merry slipped her key in the lock, sped across the hall and paused as she so often had as a child to decide which of the two circular stairways she would ascend.

It had been a perfect day. Before anyone but the servants were up, she had left the house to scurry across town for breakfast with Mike's family. Her own parents thought, if they thought at all, that she had gone shopping early; and, of course, she had the gown to prove it.

The shopping had taken scarcely more than an hour, and that was done at the end of her day. The rest of those lovely hours she had spent comparing news from Mike's letters with Mrs. Bernardo, teasing Mike's young brother, helping his sister Maria serve lunch, sitting in the comfortable living room and listening to Mr. Bernardo talk with pride about his sons in the service of his adopted country.

"Mike will be out of service in no time," she had said.

"*Si. Si.* This trouble, it is a little one for the strength of our great nation to finish soon. Then Mike will be back and, *bambina*, we shall plan such a wedding!" She loved the way he accepted her, not because of anything she was herself but because Mike loved her.

Such a wedding! Merry smiled to herself as she recalled the scene.

※　※　※

Refreshed by a brisk shower, she dressed quickly, paraded before her mirror and knew she had made a good selection. *I'll have a portrait made for Mike,* she decided.

Merry settled herself against her pillows with the little case of letters in her hand. She'd have time to read the last three—read them and dream a bit before the ball. She was very young and very contented. It had been a full day and the dream became a real one.

The upstairs maid stopped knocking and turned the handle of her door. "Miss Merry! Miss Merry, are you all right? It's eight o'clock."

"Oh!" She slipped her feet into her silver shoes and shook out her skirt. "I only leaned back for a minute, Linda. I must have napped an hour. Have I ruined my dress?"

"Not a bit of it, Miss. You didn't move a single time, from the look of you. It's lovely, Miss Merry." The girl's eyes were wide with admiration. "You'd best fix your hair and hurry. Your father sent me up."

They both understood what that meant.

Merry had just entered the great dining hall when Murphy came in, looked about in evident distress and came quickly to her side. "It's a phone call for you, Miss Merry."

"Please take the number, Murphy. I'll call back tomorrow. You know Daddy would be furious if I left now."

"I tried that, Miss. It's a lady and she sounds—upset. She said she had to talk to you right now; and if I don't get you on the phone, she'll come over. She was crying, I think, Miss Merry."

No one had heard their conversation, but Clark Johnson saw the look on his daughter's face as she turned from the old butler and ran from the room. He reached the library door just as she gave a little moan and sank in a crumpled heap by the big leather couch.

Merry opened her eyes slowly, partly because she couldn't remember what had happened and partly because she didn't want to open them at all. In the first minutes of semiconsciousness, the feeling of floating comfort was almost too much to resist; but the anxious voices dragged her back to reality. Reality was horrible; she did not want to face it.

"She'll be all right. See, she's coming around now." It was old Sam Hallack sounding professional but as usual looking like a man just in from the fields in spite of his evening clothes.

Through half-closed lashes Merry could see her mother's little white hands weaving ceaselessly back and forth against her soft satin skirt. "She probably needs a rest. Clark, we'll run down to Palm Beach and not send her back to school. Her grades have been good, and I know she's been working hard and busy with all sorts of parties."

"There now, Kitten. She'll be all right. Young girls act like fools chasing all over the country, trying to stay in school and keep up with ladies like you. We'll take her out of school this next term certainly if Sam says so and let her have a tutor if she needs one. Fool thing for her to faint; she never did before. What made her come to the phone anyway?" He didn't wait for an answer. "You go on back to our guests, Kitten. Doc will bring her around, and I'll stay to see about her."

Merry opened her eyes and tried to smile at the three of them. "I'm awake now, Daddy, but I don't want to be better." She broke into wild sobbing. "I don't want to live. He didn't have to die. He wasn't even fighting—just killed like any boy by a crazy driver. Why did he have to die?" She was sitting up now, her hands clenched against her heart.

"He?" Clark Johnson questioned as he sat down beside his elder daughter, this slip of a girl of seventeen. "Who didn't have to die?"

Merry leaned wearily against him. "Just two weeks more

and he would have been home. I could have been with him these last months if we hadn't been afraid you wouldn't let us get married. Now it doesn't matter."

"What fool talk is this? You, married? At seventeen?" The words were harsh but he changed his tone to one of deceptive sweetness. "Merry, tell me what you mean."

Suddenly the girl remembered the little stray pup she had hidden in the stables years ago. At first her father had demanded that she tell what she had done with it; then his voice had changed to one of soft persuasion, convincing her that he meant only to look at the little stray and let her keep him. When she had taken his hand and led him to the stall, chattering all the while of combing and cleaning and feeding and loving her pet, he had been silent. When he saw the dog, Clark Johnson had called the groom and ordered, "Take this thing out and shoot him. We'll have only thoroughbred dogs here."

There was no gentleness in the arms that held her now. Merry pushed away and sat looking at her father until he repeated, "Someone has died? Who?"

"Who, Merry?" Her mother repeated. "I always planned a lovely church wedding for you with a reception on the side lawn with arches of flowers for you to stand under."

Share with them her sorrow and the story of her love for Mike and his for her? They had loved each other even when they were children. What difference would arches of flowers have made if they could only have stood before a minister? If they only could have had a little apartment where she could cook for him and darn his socks. She tried to choke back the sobs because she knew her mother would never understand and there was treachery in her father's voice.

Clark's hands settled heavily on her shoulders. "Answer your mother, Merry."

"Someone I know died." Her voice was dead too, but that was all she dared say. They would not be interested in the rest—that she and Mike had talked of marriage the summer before when he was inducted into the army; and that they decided if she finished school first and he got out of service and went into his father's business, her own parents would offer less objection.

Foolish thought! The one time Mike had come to her home when her father was there, Clark had ordered him away; the scene that followed was indelibly printed in her memory. "I'll shoot him on sight if I have to," he had stormed. "You know what you've come from, Merry, an old family and a proud one. I sent that tramp away today and I want you to have nothing to do with him hereafter. Do I make myself clear?"

"You've no right to talk like that," she had tried to reason. "He's the finest boy I ever saw. He's made high grades in school. Daddy, our family may be an old and proud one, but Mike's has made a place in this country too. His father has a business as big and as important as yours, and he made it all himself. He's not a tramp. You can't say—"

Her father's face had contorted with fury. "I'll never say anything about him again. From this day on you are to forget you ever heard of that—that foreigner."

Suddenly he jerked her back to the present and the scene became somewhat clear for the first time. "If it is just 'someone,' then, my girl, we can all go back to our guests. Dry your eyes and join your crowd."

Again faintness almost overcame her; she looked at her father dully. "I only just heard. He wasn't just someone; I loved him."

"I'm sorry about your friend, Merry, but get hold of yourself and act like my daughter."

"Careful, Clark, she's had a shock." Dr. Sam spoke from his professional rank as well as his position as friend. "Don't make it any harder for her." The doctor knew the death of a casual acquaintance could not have upset the girl so much.

"Keep out of this, Sam. You are here to get her back in the dining room. Give her something. I don't believe in pampering these hysterical girls. The thing that surprises me is that Merry never acted like this before. It's as if— Merry, what was that boy to you?"

"Everything, Daddy. Absolutely everything." She stood before them, swaying slightly but her head was held high and proud. She drew herself to her full height and, at the moment, looked very like her handsome father. There was the same set to her lips, the same flashing light in her eyes. "He's the first person who ever loved me. And I loved him, and I shall love our child."

Somewhere Merry had read of someone being turned to a pillar of salt. She thought of that woman now as she watched her mother. All sorts of silly, useless things swept through her mind. Suppose her mother were so astonished she'd never move again. Might she be turned into something, too? Would her little, restless hands stay poised gracefully in midair? And what about her father? But there was no time to speculate about Clark Johnson. He looked like a madman.

"What?" It was more a growl than a word. He stormed toward his daughter with such fury that he would have struck her if it had not been for the intervention of Sam Hallack.

"Take it easy, Clark," the old doctor advised. "This little girl is heartbroken. Don't make it any worse. She needs quiet."

"Quiet! Can you be quiet about a thing like this? There'll be no fatherless waif in my family."

"It's too late for such talk. Use your head, man." Dr. Sam was stern. "Merry will have her baby, but whether or not she keeps it depends on many things."

"I want my baby, Dr. Sam. I want him more than anything in all the world, and I'll keep him. I will. I've nothing else now."

"You'll go to a home for unwed mothers, just as all of your

kind do. You'll put your baby up for adoption, and that's the end of it." Her father was pale now, almost as pale as Merry, and his voice echoed the white anger of his heart.

"No!" Merry was white and trembling as she sank back on the sofa. "You can't make me, Daddy. You don't have the right to decide about other people's lives, not even mine any longer." They were both too angry and too much alike in determination to realize they were fighting an issue they might not be able to settle themselves.

"Can't I? If you keep the child—if you refuse to keep this abominable, accursed thing quiet, I'll ruin his life. I'll plaster him with names he'll never be able to escape, and you'll wish you were never born."

He would do it, too. They all knew he never broke his word. The child, if she kept him, would have nothing but a scarred, wretched future. Clark turned to the doctor and his weeping wife. "Sam, take Kitten through that door into the back hall until I call you."

But for once Druscilla was not ready to move at his command. "Clark, darling, I want to help Merry."

"Then leave her to me."

"So many young people are foolish—you can't arrange anything for her now."

"Of course I can, love. Go with Sam. Merry will be all right."

She believed him. He had granted her every wish; surely he would do the same for their daughter. When they closed the door, Clark turned to the girl. "Now you will tell me the name of the man."

Merry read in his face the bitter warning of anger and retribution.

"I can't."

"You mean there were so many?"

"Oh, Daddy, please. All I want is to go away someplace."

"You think maybe *his* family would help you, take you in and not see you for what you are?"

"They would. I know they would."

"Who is his family?"

"Just let me go!"

"I'll let you go, but first I'll tell you what I can do. You will never mention it to anyone."

"You can't force me to be quiet."

"If you think you love this man, you'll think twice before you become responsible for his family being completely ruined. I'll wreck their careers, their business, whatever they have. They'll be paupers, disgraced, bankrupt. I can do it too. It may take a few months or even a year or two but there will be enough trouble and business failure and disgrace to turn everyone they know against them. I'd do it. You know I'd do it."

For a long moment Merry looked at him in stunned silence; then she said softly, "I don't believe you'd really be that cruel. You couldn't stand yourself if you did."

"You think not? I'll tell you this, my high-minded girl. I've set my eyes on the White House, but first I'll be in the governor's mansion. One hint of your affair would be all I'd need to stop me. I won't take the chance. I won't have it."

"If you had known him or his family you'd not be like this. Please—"

"I will please to do as I please." Of one thing now Clark was sure: whoever it was with whom Merry had become involved was not someone he knew. He read into her statement about knowing the boy and his family all that she had meant to imply. Had he been the son of his own friends or acquaintances, they too would have heard of his death. Perhaps it was someone she had met while at school. Let it go; it couldn't matter. She'd soon understand that. But his next step was to convince her. "So you don't think I'd carry this through? Remember last year when the Howell Jenkins firm broke? Do you recall what happened to the grandfather?"

"No. No." The protest was involuntary because in her mind's eye, Merry could see again the blaring headlines. Howell Jenkins' daughter was her good friend. The papers blared the collapse of the firm and soon broadcast the news of the people who lost fortunes due to mismanagement of their funds by the firm. Then there was the story of the heart attack which struck the founder of the business. They must be true, the things her father was trying to imply. The reporters had made much of the fact that Clark Johnson was the last to talk with H. P. Jenkins. Minutes after he left, the old gentleman rang for his secretary, but collapsed as she came in the door.

"Won't you have mercy, Daddy? I've never caused you any trouble. You'd never have to hear of me again."

"It's your decision, not mine."

Merry was broken at that moment and knew it. She moaned, then burst forth wildly. "I'll hate you every hour of my life and every day I shall pray that everything you ever want will be snatched away from you."

"Pray! You against me? What good do you think that would do?" He opened the door to admit his wife and the doctor.

Druscilla Johnson was weeping. "I can't stand it, Clark. She's so young and so pretty. I want my child to be happy."

"She'll be all right, Kitten. Give her time and she'll get over this."

But Druscilla knew her daughter wasn't all right. It was more than grief that put the horrible mark on her face, the terror in her eyes. She moved forward, her arms outstretched in a rare demonstration of affection, but her husband stopped her.

"Druscilla, you must trust me. Sam and I know what we are doing. You must not upset her more than she is already."

"I'll have to go away, Clark. I could never see Merry being miserable for so long." She was beating her soft fists against his chest.

He took out his handkerchief and brushed aside her tears, smiled and soothed her. "Of course you can go away. Why not the Riviera? You could take Marcia along and she could do some sketching under the young artist we met last winter."

"But Merry is still such a child, Clark." She turned to that child. "Merry, I'll take you with me. Life is much simpler on the Continent."

"No!" Clark was almost stern. "Kitten, you would only hurt her chances at a new life. Take Marcia and leave Merry to me."

"I'll do it. And when we come home, poor Merry will be all right and we can have her debut during the Christmas holidays just as we planned." She leaned over and kissed Merry and allowed herself to be led from the room.

As Clark closed the door behind them, a crowd of young people gathered around them.

"What's the matter with Merry?"

"Will she be all right?"

"I never knew her to faint before."

Clark Johnson even managed a laugh. "Merry will be all right. She was a bit tired when she came home from school. The plane ran into heavy rain and was delayed. She's been running in high since she landed, and who knows what junk you youngsters eat! Doc will take care of her. Kitten and I are going to have a waltz before the noise begins." Almost gaily he swept his wife onto the floor, and no one watching them would have known that Clark Johnson was frightened and fighting for self-control.

"I don't think I can dance, Clark; I'm far too upset. I don't know what to do. I think I must lie down."

"Nonsense, Kitten. You've never deserted me yet. This party may not be ruined after all. Smile at me, love. Merry will come to her senses; she'll have to. We'll consider this no more of a tragedy in a few months than if it had never happened. We'll just say she's sick, needs a good rest, and send her off to someplace Sam will know about. She'll come out of it fine. If she were a boy, we'd not take this too seriously."

"Oh, Clark—"

"These things can be hushed up. Brace up, Kitten. You are too beautiful this minute to waste on a fit of emotion."

She laughed up at her husband as he had intended. Flattery, gallantry and soft music always lifted Druscilla out of any depression. He had married her because she took the world lightly and all its troubles were none of her concern. He had kept her untouched by worries almost all of their twenty years together. Clark had no intention of his wife changing now. No. She was at her loveliest and he'd keep her so.

2

Clark's Command

BACK IN THE LIBRARY, Merry almost stopped her sobbing. "They don't even care, Dr. Sam. They never cared about me."

It was true and there was no use denying it. Clark and his wife lived only for each other. She was his doll wife and the rest of the world only served as props for their life together. Even their daughters were merely conversation pieces to complement their own lives. Nothing must spoil the picture, no matter what.

Clark Johnson had inherited much of his fortune; the rest came by skillful management. Now that he was rising to political power in the state and had even been mentioned as candidate for the governor's office, he was determined to have that coveted position no matter who had to be swept out of his way.

"I don't want to stay here, Dr. Sam," Merry continued. "I'll never want to stay here again. I don't want to see my mother packing her bags and hurrying away from me as if I were a plague. I can't bear to have my father—" Her voice trailed off, for there was no point in saying more. From long experience, the doctor knew Clark was as ruthless as any man unless there was something to gain.

"You don't know your Aunt Margaret very well, do you, Merry?"

"Oh, no. She and Mother don't have the same interests—and—were you thinking she might—?"

"Not only might, my dear. She would welcome you. She is very interested in her nieces. I know because we work together in her clinic, and she always asks me about you and Marcia."

"But now, Dr. Sam?"

"Now she's the one you can really trust. Tell her everything and let her help you decide about yourself and your child. I'll stand by you whatever you want to do, and I know Margaret will too."

"I'd like to talk to Aunt Margaret, but she can't help me really. I want to keep my baby but—Daddy—"

"Be reasonable, Merry. There's nothing Clark can do to hurt you. He's not all powerful, and you'll find that out sooner or later. Let me help you."

A sob was her only answer.

"You lie there, Merry. I'll make a call and then we'll be on our way."

"Are you sure she'll have me?"

"I'm sure and, my child, I don't know what your father said to you. I've no idea of the threat he used, but don't make a decision now."

The big, white-haired man opened the door, beckoned to a servant, and said quietly, "Peter, fetch a maid and do it quickly. Then when you get her, you come back too." People moved when Dr. Hallack gave orders, in or out of the hospital.

In a matter of seconds he was directing the maid. "Miss Merry is in the library. Go in and look after her." To the man he said, "Stand here, Peter, until I come back, and don't let anyone go in at all."

"Not even Mr. or Mrs. Johnson, Doctor?"

"Not anyone, Peter. Doctor's orders. And you had better see to it that Miss Merry stays here until I come back. She might think she's well enough to go out on her own. I'd rather take her. These youngsters don't know the limit of their own strength. It's not what it was when I was a boy."

He went to the phone in Clark's study. "Margaret, may I bring someone to you tonight?" He spoke as he had spoken to her for the last twenty years, no preamble, no hesitancy, just what was on his heart. Explanations were never necessary between them. "Right now, Margaret." This time he did hesitate and the woman knew by the tremor of his voice that he was struggling with unusual emotion. "It's Merry. I'll bring her over to you, my dear. Clark is giving her a rough time. The girl's in real trouble, and Clark will have none of it. I'd like to break his neck. . . . I know, Margaret, but the boy is dead and she just found out. . . . She needs you. . . . In about an hour, and you'd better have Becky heat some broth. . . . Good-bye, my love."

On his way out of the study, Dr. Hallack cornered Murphy, whose eyes showed his great concern. "Have Miss Merry's bags packed for a long visit, Murphy. She'll need some of all types of clothing probably. I'll give you twenty minutes."

"There's no one to do it, Dr. Hallack. We're still busy serving and Mr. Clark would be irritated—"

"Murphy, leave Clark to me. Get someone to pack Miss Merry's bags. *Now!*"

"There is no one, sir."

It was that moment Clark Johnson chose to enter the hall from the brightly lighted dining room. "Murphy, this is the first time you've ever neglected your duties."

"It may not be the last." Dr. Sam spoke between clenched teeth. "Murphy is either going to have one of the maids pack Merry's bags or do it himself. And now!"

"Merry isn't going anyplace tonight, Sam. Neither is this party going to be any more disrupted than it has been. Come on into the ballroom where you belong."

"You fool!" The older man laid a heavy hand on his host's

shoulder and the grip brought pain to Clark's face as he jerked away. "That girl is heartbroken, and you have almost killed her with what you said when you sent Druscilla and me out. You talk of this party! You either send a maid to pack for her or I'll go in and create a scene this town won't forget."

With a string of smothered oaths, Clark turned to Murphy who stood by, white-faced and shaken. "Get Belinda. Turn her over to Dr. Hallack. And, Murphy, not a word about this to anyone."

"Yes, Mr. Clark."

The doctor's car was at the door when he came out of the great stone house, half carrying Merry. She crouched in her corner as they left the circular drive and joined the rather heavy traffic.

Looking at her briefly while they waited at a stoplight, the doctor cleared his throat and said, "You know, Merry, this doesn't mean the end of the world for you. You are young, and life doesn't stop because of one heartache. The best thing is for you to set your mind on what you'll be doing eight months from now and plan—"

"I'll plan only what I can do to hurt my father. I can spend this time thinking of what I can do to ruin him." The girl's voice was dry and bitter.

"You listen to your aunt. She'll be glad and able to help you find happiness if anyone can."

"No one can help me, Dr. Sam. Besides, I don't want the kind of help I think you mean. I just want to go someplace and make a life for my baby. But there isn't anyplace I can do it; there's no place to go."

"You aren't alone, child. You have your aunt and me."

"Oh, I wish, I wish—but what he said—"

"Tell me, Merry. What did your father say?"

"No," she moaned. "I don't want—I can't talk about it."

✿   ✿   ✿

Margaret Johnson was as different from her brother as two people can be. The spacious apartment she shared with Becky, her housekeeper, was both simple and luxurious; Margaret could give the most unpretentious place an air of splendor.

She took Merry in her arms and felt the stiffness in the girl's tense body.

"Why, Aunt Margaret, you have tears in your eyes."

"Yes, Merry, I'm so glad to have you here."

"Dr. Sam told you?"

"Yes. And right now you are where you belong."

"You really mean it?" And the girl seemed to melt in her arms.

"I really do, Merry. Now we'll give you some broth and put you to bed, and tomorrow will be time enough to make plans."

" 'She gave them some broth without any bread, spanked them all soundly and put them to bed,' " Merry chanted, a faint smile on her trembling lips. "No spanking?"

"No spanking, Merry. I'll take you to your room and get you settled for the night. Will you stay for coffee and cake, Sam?"

"I'll stay forever by your fireside if you'll let me, Margaret." Merry wondered briefly at his seriousness as she watched him settle down in the deep leather chair and reach for a magazine.

An hour later when Margaret came back into her living room, she sank on the couch with a sigh. "It's as if she had always come to me in time of trouble, Sam. She talked as freely and with as much love as if—as if she had been running in and out of my life daily."

"She trusted you at once; I could see it. Poor little kid. She never had a real home, Margaret. She's never known parental love. She just recognizes in you the love she's never had and always needed. She's under Clark's spell right now, but maybe you can break through that; maybe you can make her see he's not so powerful. But, if not, have you thought of what you'll do with her?"

"Yes. I had halfway decided to go away for a rest myself, a rest and a chance to do some papers and prepare a few talks for the clubwomen who let me come in now and then to tell them about my girls and the clinic. What would you say to my taking Merry with me across the state to a home that's run by Beverly Anders? Remember when she visited me last winter for a few weeks? You took us to dinner and to that wonderful concert afterward."

"Yes, I remember Beverly. Straitlaced old maid, if you ask me."

"Shame, Sam. You did everything you could to shock her. She was my roommate for two years and she's—dear."

"Everyone's dear to you, but go on. You probably planned it all on your way down the hall."

"Not exactly, but there are some ways you can help. For one thing, I think Clark and Druscilla will either have to become compassionate or leave Merry strictly alone. Of course it will be better for her and for the child if she will let him be adopted. It will be better still if she never sees the baby, but that decision can come later. Sam, she's so very young and she's feeling terribly alone. Merry knows her father a bit better right now than she ever did before."

"She doesn't know the extent the man would go to, or she would run away and hide in a slum. Clark is ruthless. I hope she never finds out how ruthless."

"Be that as it may, they'll never help her. They never have. She has no faith to lean on, and evidently pinned all of her hopes and dreams on this boy. Clark must not hurt her anymore. That's up to you, Sam. You can pull your professional rank."

"I pulled it tonight by kidnapping your niece, and I can

pull it again. But then, I never did quake when Clark roared, like most of his family and friends."

They talked on and on until almost every detail was arranged as far as they could plan without Merry being there too. It was nothing new for Dr. S. A. Hallack and Miss Margaret Johnson to confer about other people's problems, nor was it new for the man to leave with great reluctance.

3

Midnight Tryst

MERRY, LEFT ALONE in her aunt's comfortable guest room, tried to lie quietly and rest, but she couldn't. If she could only shake off the tight despair encompassing her like a strangling garment, she might find peace. She had felt warmed and comforted and almost protected when she saw her aunt's loving smile. In her arms she had wept like the frightened child she was. But now, alone, no feeling of comfort remained. She had no more tears to shed, only the bleak sense of loss and fear.

For most of her life she had thought of no future that did not include Mike. There had always been the letters and phone calls to bridge the gap when they were separated by trips she took with her parents. She had gone out with other boys because she had no alternative in the set in which her family placed her. Merry had even told Mike she didn't mind if he went with other girls just as long as he didn't consider getting serious about any of them.

She remembered the last time she had said it. Was it three years ago? Yes, it must have been. She was almost fifteen then and Mike just eighteen, ready to graduate from high school. He had invited her to the prom. "If I can," she had promised. "But if I can't, you must ask someone else."

Then it was they settled forever the question of their love.

"I'll never want anyone else but you, Merry. You know that, don't you?"

She did, of course. The prom was only one of their many times together. When her father asked about her dates, and that was rare, Merry left the house with another boy, but it was always Mike who brought her home.

Without even talking about it, her own crowd and Mike's seemed to enjoy the conspiracy.

The girl couldn't rest. It wasn't true that he wouldn't come home to her; it must be a mistake. She said the words over and over until she almost believed them. Then Merry remembered Mrs. Bernardo's voice as she spoke over the phone.

Merry wanted to run out of Aunt Margaret's comfortable apartment, speed across town and throw herself into the arms of Mike's mother. She wanted to tell her that she, Merry, had a right to be there grieving with his family, the greatest right in the world. But, no. She would never be able to tell them that she was going to have Mike's baby.

She wept again—dry, rasping sobs which could scarcely be stifled in her pillow. Then a decision came. She would go to Mike's mother. She would stay with the family as many hours as she could stand to.

The tears began again when Merry thought of the plans she must make. In only a few days she had intended to ask them if she could live in their home to wait for Mike's leave when they would be married—and then to stay on with them if Mike were sent overseas. She had planned to be with them when Mike's son was born. Now they would never know about Mike's child. Oh, she loved them so much and she could never tell them. She should have been a part of their large close-knit family; instead, she was just—Mike's girl-friend.

Her father! Merry shuddered at the memory of his face and the lack of understanding, the scorn and hate she had seen there. He would do every miserable thing he had threatened if she did not obey him.

She picked up the precious little leather box from her overnight bag, got the key from her purse and opened it. She stood, hesitating, looking down at her treasury of letters. She touched them caressingly, then drew from the bottom of the case one rather large envelope. Carefully the girl unfolded a marriage license and read it over and over as she had many times before. It had been in Mike's possession until his last leave; she had carried it with her ever since, but she could do that no longer. Merry had read of court records being changed or destroyed. This bit of paper was the only clue to the name her father wanted. Out of sheer pride he would not ask anyone about her dates. The least said, the least anyone would suspect had always been his adage. She was glad she hadn't mentioned Mike's name. Her father would not be able to hurt him or his family. She would not even tell Aunt Margaret or Dr. Sam.

Someday when she finished her work of vengeance, she would reclaim her child. At the moment the paper in her hand was all the comfort Merry had, but she would forgo even that to prevent her father from finding out the name of the little town and the courthouse where the permanent record of their hope rested. Mike had wanted to go immediately to a minister; she had argued a later date would be better, especially if her parents went on a cruise as they usually did during the winter. How foolish, how foolish!

She crumpled that piece of paper and clutched it so tightly that her nails bit into the soft flesh of her palms without her even knowing it. Once again tears streamed unheeded down her cheeks as she remembered his last furlough.

Soon after he left, a letter came announcing, "I'll be home on leave for a month immediately after Christmas. There will be no arguments this time, for I've decided that is when we'll add a new Mrs. Bernardo to our family."

There had been other letters, but now there would be no more. The girl stood by the marble-topped table with a burning match in her hand. Slowly she lowered the paper to it; quickly the flames left a small pile of ashes in the tray.

Then Merry Johnson, the girl who had everything money can buy, went to stand by the darkened windows to watch dawn break over the sleepy river.

❀   ❀   ❀

She told her aunt the next morning, "I'm going out for the day."

"I'll drive you."

"Please, no. Not today. I want to take a cab and, Aunt Margaret, don't worry if I'm late getting back, and don't be surprised if I come back at once. I don't know—I really don't know—how long I'll be."

"Darling child, talk to me. What can I do for you?" There was a long pause. "Where are you going? Don't pay any attention to what your father said. He can't do anything to you now."

"I have to have a little time away—to think about some personal matters. Today I'll probably not think of Daddy. I couldn't."

"I can't let you go out alone."

Then Merry saw the stark worry in her aunt's eyes. She knew Margaret feared she would do something to destroy herself. It was a pitiful laugh, but Merry managed to say rather lightly, "Don't worry about me, Aunt Margaret; I'll take very good care of myself. I'm going to see to it that nothing happens to me until I finish with my daddy."

"My dear, you will only be hurt if you let this bitterness take possession of you. Don't think of what Clark threatened. From the moment I told Sam to bring you to me, I knew we had a battle of some kind on our hands. My dear, I'm prepared to take care of you in any way I can."

"Thank you, but—"

"But what? Do you want to tell me about him?"

Merry moved her hand as if to brush aside the whole conversation, but after a slight pause, spoke gently, almost as if
to herself. "I want to but there isn't much to tell now. I
knew his whole family—" Her voice broke, but she continued
with a little sob. "I know them very well, but— They are fine
and good and real. We used to go there lots of times when
Mums and Daddy were out of town. I've been to operas often but sometimes in the evenings in their home, they put on
whole operas just for fun. When they had parties, they
weren't like the ones Mother and Daddy have. People go
to their house to enjoy each other."

"Do you want to talk to the boy's family? Do you want
them to know?"

"Not about the baby—not now." For a moment she looked
as if she might faint, but when she spoke again there was no
emotion in her voice at all. "Oh, Aunt Margaret, all the
world could know if we had only married, and Daddy
couldn't make me give up my child."

"Merry—"

"Even now they would want the baby and could manage
something, but I won't even tell you his name—although I
want to. I don't want anyone to be able to tell Daddy."

"As if I would."

"Of course not, Aunt Margaret, but sometimes people let
things slip. Let's not speak of it anymore. I'll be back sometime."

It was late when she returned to the quiet apartment,
scarcely able to move toward her room. Margaret put her
arms around the slender girl and led her to the soft bed.
She and Becky undressed and put her between the sheets as
if she were the sick child she appeared to be; and it was as if
Merry did not know they were there.

Long after Becky had gone to her room, Margaret sat in a

small rocker beside the bed. Finally she asked, "Is there anything I can do for you? Anything at all?"

"No, not tonight. But I may run away for another day." She wanted to cry out, "Come with me," but her tryst had to be a lonely one. Then the sobs came—great choking sobs—and Margaret rocked her in her arms until the girl was finally quiet again and able to say in a thin attempt at well-being, "I'll be fine now. I'd like to be alone for a while."

The woman left reluctantly only after she said she'd leave her door open and Merry was to call if she wanted anything.

Margaret did not ask questions. Hard as it was she knew her part now was to stand by. She dared not pry into this hour of agony. Of course she wondered where her niece had gone and what she had said to explain her presence.

She could not know Merry felt like a traitor by her silence. She had sat by Mike's mother and wept with her. She had tried to console the older woman only to have the comfort of her soft, plump arms break her own self-control. Then she looked at Mrs. Bernardo's gentle face with the tender eyes, at Mr. Bernardo's toil-worn hands; at Maria rocking her small son; at Josef, the young brother whom Mike had called his best pal. She looked at the older brothers and sisters as they moved in and out of that house of mourning. This grief would always be with them. It would lessen, yes, but the depth of their love and family feeling was so great they would always mourn for the one not there. She could add no greater burden.

She remembered Margaret's words of the morning, "You have a right to turn to them if you think you should. I want to keep you with me, Merry, and help you in the way I think best. But you must decide. And if his family would be a comfort and would understand—"

Understand? She thought they would, even if they did not approve because they were very religious people. However, they would forgive and would never be like her father. Com-

fort? Comfort! Yes. It would be a great comfort. But would
having Mike's child in their home compensate for the complete business and financial loss that her father promised?
They had had poverty, the elder Bernardos, when they first
came to this country. It had not mattered. They were young
then and strong, but now— No!

When Merry had left them that day, she knew her decision
was irrevocable. They had each kissed her and said endear-
ing words that tore her heart. The hardest part was when
Josef, whom she loved to tease, put his arms around her and
said, "You will always be my sister, Merry. Mike would have
it so."

❋   ❋   ❋

Tuesday she did not slip unnoticed into the cathedral;
someone had been watching for her. The young girl in her
simple black dress was led to the place reserved for the
family. She alone knew there should have been a ring on her
finger to proclaim her right to be there.

4

Margaret's Plan

Two days later, Merry, who had moved as if in a stupor, asked, "Where can I go, Aunt Margaret?"

"I had planned to take a vacation, dear, and there would be nothing strange or especially newsworthy about my taking a favorite niece and going away for a rest. I'll take an apartment near where you'll be staying with a friend of mine."

"You mean you've already arranged it?"

"No, there's little arranging to do. I'll simply have to write to Miss Anders and tell her we need to come if that's what you decide. We could leave as soon as we have her reply. In fact, we might ask her to phone. Meanwhile, we'll pack and prepare to disappear for a few months. Is that what you really think you are going to do, Merry?"

The girl chose to ignore the question. "How can you be so sure, so very sure, of what her answer will be?"

"Because she's a Christian, too. We have the same Master."

The girl said quickly, "I don't know what you mean."

"You see, Merry, when I was a little girl, I found out that God loved me and wanted me to serve Him. I learned that He is all-powerful, merciful and loving. I try to follow Him and seek His will in all I do. I can't begin to tell you how happy I've been in knowing the Lord as my Saviour and

Friend. Beverly Anders does too. There are so many things we don't have to explain to each other or ask each other. Being with another Christian is like being with one's other self. Our reactions, our motives, our desires are based on the Lord and His Word. It's the greatest freedom, Merry. I want you to know my Lord and Saviour, too. He will make your burden light. He will give you peace."

"I never thought of God as having a personal interest in people. I mean, of caring what happens to individuals. I don't believe He does."

"When you went to Sunday school, Merry, didn't you learn John 3:16? 'For God so loved the world, that he gave his only begotten Son, that whosoever believeth in him should not perish, but have everlasting life.' "

"Don't you know we rarely went to Sunday school except for the few weeks we spent with Grandmother at the beach some summers? Then *she* told us strange things about God. I believe she tried to teach Marcia and me some verses, but we were never there long enough to learn anything. She wanted us to spend the summer with her the year I was ten; but she died just before vacationtime, and Mother and Daddy had to cancel their European trip because of it. Later that year they did take their trip and sent me to a lovely camp. I can't remember where Marcia went."

"Merry, will you listen while I read to you about God's love?"

"Tell me something first, Aunt Margaret. Daddy is your brother. Did he hear what you want to read to me?"

"Yes, dear. Our mother taught us both."

"But he didn't believe?"

"He would never accept the fact that he owed anything to any person—not even to God. No, Merry, he would never listen with his heart."

"Have you tried to talk with him about God?"

"Many times."

"What did he say?"

Margaret shuddered slightly as she recalled her brother's words of blasphemy. "You go on with your sanctified, selfless life if you want to, Margaret. It doesn't seem to hurt you any. But *me!* I've got other plans."

To his daughter, Margaret simply replied, "He would not listen."

"Then it wouldn't make any difference to him how I feel any more than it made the other night. He wouldn't especially care if I began to believe in—something. He never has cared anyway."

"Of course he cares, Merry, in his way. You are his daughter and a very beautiful and talented girl. He's probably only hurt and upset that you didn't let him give you away in a beautiful wedding."

"He really doesn't care what happens to me, Aunt Margaret. He could help me now if I meant anything to him at all. But I don't. I don't want to talk about him. Let's not."

Before Margaret could protest further that she too wanted to talk about something else, Merry got up and left the room. How could she ever make this embittered girl see that she wanted to talk only about Jesus, the Saviour, and not about Clark Johnson and his rejection of God?

❁　❁　❁

Later that week Margaret sat at her desk in the downtown clinic where she presided at least three days a week. "Sam," she said to the busy doctor, "would you care to drive me home and have dinner with Merry and me?"

"Are you sure you feel all right, Margaret?"

"Oh, Sam—will you?"

"You don't often ask me, you know. Of course I'll drive you home or anyplace. Let's make this a short day and a long drive home." He could have used the same words twenty years ago. Perhaps he did.

But it wasn't a short day. None of them was, there at the

clinic. And when they finally started toward Margaret's apartment, she had the feeling their work had been left half done. A few more on the staff, a larger building, another full-time personal worker, and they would be able to get out more into the neighborhoods and answer some of the calls they now had to turn over to the regular charities.

"Sensible thing to do all along," Dr. Sam had grumbled again and again. "I don't see how I got tied up with charity work on my afternoons off. I should have better sense."

"We need you, Sam, but you know you can stop anytime you want."

"Yes, and you'd get another doctor overnight."

"Maybe not. We've had to do without a full-time doctor often enough. You know we started here first to help mothers of young babies; we only wanted to tell them about Jesus. That's all I was really equipped to do with Lois as my only full-time worker. But with your help and the nurses you've provided, we've had a wonderful time. Confess, my dear. You think so too, don't you?"

"You call me 'my dear,' and I'll think anyplace is wonderful. Oh, come on, Margaret, you couldn't get rid of me on Tuesday and Thursday afternoons if you had me locked in jail. I'd break the bars with my bare hands."

There was much these two could say and much they left unsaid.

"I can't let her go on like this, Sam. She paces up and down in her room, and she isn't sleeping much at night. When I go in to talk with her, she's always animated now. And, in spite of my counseling experience, she has me talking about the things *she* wants to discuss. And we avoid all the important subjects she needs to settle for herself; she doesn't talk about the boy at all. I can't get her to go out anymore. All of her emotions and all her thoughts are involved in love for the baby and hate for her father."

"You've always been a woman of great faith. Can't you tell her about your God?"

"That's the strangest and hardest part for me, Sam. I've talked with many about God's saving grace and great love; I've told them about the blessed Lord Jesus. But when I try to talk with this girl—this precious niece of mine—she won't listen."

"How does she avoid it?"

"At first she said, 'I can't believe in your God. If He is so loving and good, why does He let people be as unhappy as I am?' So I tried to explain how we can't always see why things happen the way they do, but if we love God, we know all things work for our good. Sam, she simply answered, 'Aunt Margaret, I don't like to say this because I know it will hurt you, but I don't even *like* God.' She began to weep then, and I tried to tell her that He loves her. She interrupted to say, 'I can't imagine God speaking to a human heart, not to mine anyway.'"

She didn't relate it all to her companion but Margaret had continued then to talk to her niece. "Sometimes we close our eyes to His beauty and our ears to His voice, Merry. Let me tell you how I heard Him call me."

"It isn't that I'm not interested in you, Aunt Margaret. It's just that I'm tired, and hearing about your God only makes me feel worse. Do you mind if I rest a while now?"

There was nothing more Margaret could say. In telling the doctor about it, she said, "Truly, Sam, she was almost shaking. It has been something like that every time we discuss anything more personal than the weather." She knew he was not the one to advise her but she asked anyway, "Sam, what can I do to help her?"

"I expect I've felt just as helpless every time I've seen a patient I'm not sure about. Those that fall into the regular patterns aren't hard to diagnose, but this girl is one of the different ones. She's had to live in her own self-sufficiency since she was out of the nursery, and that was much too soon. I've watched her all of her life and I've loved her as if she were my own, more than any of the other children that have been in my care. But the way her life has been, she was allowed little opportunity to lean on any adult very much."

"How could he do it to her, Sam? How could he leave Merry and Marcia completely out of his life—his and Druscilla's?"

"It wasn't hard. Druscilla has never been anything but a pampered, beautiful pet. I doubt that she's spent more than a few hours with either of the girls all their lives. We're all different, my dear. I can't explain Clark. I can't even explain myself." His laugh wasn't what he had intended it to be. In fact, little he did or said around Margaret turned out the way he wanted it to. It seemed that all of his life, Sam Hallack had been trying to make Margaret understand that their love for each other was all that mattered.

"We can do anything, we can accomplish anything in the world together," he had promised one summer night. "Anything, my darling, if you'll only marry me. Our love is all that is important."

Margaret had laid her hand in his and, after a moment in which she seemed to be listening, said softly, "Sam, I do love you; I suppose I always have. I know there will never be anyone else. But until the day you can believe in my Saviour, I won't marry you. I can't. I can only pray you will find the happiness I have!"

So through the years they had often worked side by side. They had talked of many things—everything, really—and had reached many important decisions. Sam sat through hundreds of good gospel sermons, but he insisted a man of science could not be stupid enough to accept the virgin birth, much less the teaching that the blood of one Man could save sinners.

Now as they neared the apartment building where Margaret made her home in the winter, she said quietly, "It's strange, isn't it, Sam, that the very people I want most to know my Lord won't believe."

                    ✿   ✿   ✿

Becky's dinners were always festive. This night Dr. Sam exerted himself as he knew so well how to do. They were laughing at his stories of some patients in the midst of their meal when Merry suddenly asked, "What is my father telling people about me?"

"Pretty much what I expected. He said you became ill with a virus and had reacted poorly to the drugs. I ordered you to give up everything—including school—for a few months. A few days later he issued a statement very cleverly through the biggest gossip in his set. He said you had been invited to spend the time of your convalescence with your aunt. Your mother had also been smitten by the same illness and was ordered to take a sea voyage, but you were too weak from your bout of Asiatic flu to go with her. How's that for Clark's imagination?"

"I hate him! I hate him!" Merry said between clenched teeth. "Someday I'll make him pay for everything he's doing to me. Hasn't anyone asked you anything, Dr. Sam?"

"Of course. I feel like I'm being interviewed by the press when I go to the club these days."

"And you say?"

"Simply that you were finally responding, but slowly, and you need complete rest. Your father is concerned and is keeping informed of your condition. I said your mother is making a rapid recovery but needs a change of scene. Some people have had the flu harder than others, and it is apparent your resistance was very low. All right, Merry?"

"You've always been wonderful, Dr. Sam. I never realized how wonderful until right now. If we are to leave tomorrow, Aunt Margaret, I think I'll go and put a few things in a bag and leave the rest in your closet. I might want some of them again."

"Either Becky or I could do it."

"No, thank you. I'm going to learn to do a number of things alone. This is the beginning."

"I shall miss you, Margaret," Dr. Sam said much later as they stood at the door.

"Take a trip, Sam. Come to see us in a few months."

"If I can wait months. Will you write to me, Margaret?"

"Yes, Sam. Will you answer and not dictate your letters?"

"I'll try to remember that." Once he had dictated part of a letter to Margaret.

In a few minutes he was gone and Margaret smiled at the ritual of their leave-taking. How many times had she gone away and promised to write with the same words? Sometimes she thought it was better to be away and write than to talk to Sam. He would read and think about her letters and argue back across the miles. He rarely disagreed with her faith face to face, even though she would have welcomed some verbal disagreement. At least she would know if he still thought the same old way.

Margaret knelt by her window a long time and prayed until she finally simply knelt there and waited—waited for the assurance of the strength she would need to help her young kinswoman. Before she went to bed, the soft snow had almost covered the streets below and the great street-cleaning machines were already at work. It would be slow driving tomorrow, but then—they were in no hurry.

Margaret slept a deep untroubled sleep.

5

Lady-in-Waiting

THE REST OF THE WINTER MONTHS passed swiftly, with Margaret settled in her small apartment near the home for unwed mothers where Merry waited. To this woman, there were not enough hours in the day to accomplish all the self-appointed tasks she had before her.

To Merry, encompassed in a shroud of bitterness and revenge, the activities of the home were something to be endured—something to pass through as one does a dark unattractive street as quickly as possible without becoming a part of it. In addition to her studies, she was learning to mend, sew, make beds, clean her room, scrub. These things she did because she had to. In addition, she read to fill the empty hours that had formerly been spent at the theater, or playing bridge or dancing. It was the first time she had been in a manless world, but even that had not registered to the lovely girl who had so long been accustomed to flattery and praise.

She didn't scorn the girls who were there because of their own folly or weakness; she simply didn't seem any more aware of them than she was of the simple furniture or the plain food.

Merry spoke little unless it was to answer a direct question. And more than once Miss Anders, veteran social worker and accomplished Christian counselor, said to her friend sadly, "Margaret, she's the hardest to reach I've ever had. She will *not* hear. I think you should have taken her on to Maggie; she's more apt to know what to do."

They laughed even in that serious moment when they thought of Maggie, the third member of their college trio. Together they had trained for the work of helping wayward, unfortunate girls, as well as needy men and women. Even with the same Bible school training, their approach was so different that they marveled that the results were the same.

"I thought of Maggie," Margaret admitted, "but I prayed about it and felt this was the place to bring her. Beverly, I prayed hard enough before the final decision, and I know this is the answer. I'm willing to wait."

"You won't have to wait too much longer, I hope. Well, I must go back. I hate to think of your leaving in a few weeks, Margaret. Having you here has been a blessing to me. Invite us all down to your house on the beach this summer—to be pampered, as usual. And, Margaret, don't hesitate to act if you should decide to take Merry away from me."

June came in with a rush of heat, followed by two weeks of balmy glorious days. Merry knew she would soon have to let her family know what she had decided to do with her future. Actually she had little choice. Her father expected her to go on to school in the fall. All right. She would. What he did not know, what he would not know, was that she would go with a real determination to study. She would equip herself so well that she would be able to fight or spoil everything he would ever try to do politically.

Merry would soon be independent; she would have a large estate that had been left in trust by an uncle. It would be hers in three years. Then in her own car, she would speed just enough to get in the headlines; she would appear to drink just enough to cause loud talk; she would run with the fastest crowds so the gossip columnists would keep her name in print; and Clark Johnson's political future would be hurt. He could do nothing to stop her.

Merry rarely went beyond that possibility, but it was a satisfaction to dream of the day of revenge. Meanwhile she would study political science so that her comments on government and her father's own political platforms would be clever, respected. How she could ruin him she did not know fully, but there would always be many to help her—if she could prepare herself properly, if she were capable—and she would be.

Daisy, her roommate, was the only one who broke through Merry's icy reserve or could penetrate the clouds of darkness surrounding her. Probably that was because Daisy was completely a child of nature, a happy extrovert and an incomparable optimist.

✿   ✿   ✿

It was after breakfast one day and the chores were done.

"Man, this is living!" Daisy put an impulsive arm around Merry. "You know, honey, I just know from the way you talk and the books you read and the clothes you wear, you ain't never had it so hard before. What I can't figure about you is—well—you seem so sure of yourself and yet—"

"Let's take a walk, Daisy. We'll go see the beauties of the countryside and come back starving for lunch."

"You know, I'd kind of like to keep my kid," Daisy said as she sank down at the foot of a giant maple. "It would be sort of nice and I'd like to have a little girl and dress her all up in ruffles and laces and let her wear satin petticoats and go to parties." She laughed with sudden self-conscious embarrassment. "But my kid wouldn't have nothin' like that. She'd be lucky to have three squares a day."

"Isn't there any way you can keep your baby?"

"No. Bud says we'll get married as soon as I get out of here if I let the kid go. He don't want no babies with a bad start."

"But if it's his child—"

"You *are* an innocent. Sure it's his but everybody'd know

we shouldn't have had him so soon. But Bud wants to get someplace in the world. Anyhow, it sometimes makes me kinda sad. Don't you feel a little bad about givin' yours up?"

"Yes, Daisy." The words were half sob. "I don't like to think of it. Shall we go back now?"

She *didn't* like to think of it but there were no hours of the day or night that Merry didn't think of the child she must give up and of her father who was forcing her to do it.

If Mike had lived, he would have been the one to whom she could have turned. He would have had the right to care for them both.

That night she could not stay in her bed or in the room with Daisy's radio humming softly past the curfew hour and far into the night.

With her plain robe clinging to her cumbersome figure, she walked down the corridor to the side door. *If I could only run and walk, and walk or run away—but there is no place to run,* she thought for the hundredth time. *Father would find me. He'd find me so no one else would be the first to know about me. Why didn't I just disappear when I first knew?*

"Where are you going, Merry?" It was the happy little night nurse who flitted about the old mansion like a fairy child.

"I want to walk, Miss Ellen. I couldn't sleep and I *couldn't* stay in bed any longer."

"How about some hot chocolate with me? I'll let you in the kitchen and you can start it while I turn in my report."

"I'm sorry." Merry's eyes were more troubled. "I wouldn't know how to begin. I've never made hot chocolate; I've never cooked anything. I'm to have kitchen duty next."

The young nurse tucked her chart into a drawer of the desk by the door. "Come, I'll show you how."

With steaming cups before them, Miss Ellen put her hand

over Merry's. "Would talking it over help you any, Merry? I'd love to do something, you know."

In a burst of confidence completely foreign to her mode of life, Merry sobbed, "I'm grateful but there isn't anything anyone can do. There is only one person who could help me, and he has no heart. If I were wise, I'd probably pretend nothing matters; but it does. Oh, it matters a great deal. I want to keep my baby, Miss Ellen." Great choking sobs shook the girl. "There's no one to care."

"Someone *does* care, Merry. Someone cared enough to die for you."

"You mean the baby's father? He didn't die for me; he loved me. Oh, he did love me and I him, but he didn't die for me."

"No, I know he didn't. I mean the Lord Jesus Christ, God's Son."

Merry lifted her head to look at Miss Ellen. "I know He was crucified by the religious leaders of His day, but He couldn't have died for me, Miss Ellen. I never knew Him." Her eyes were filled with unalterable sadness.

"So many people can say that, Merry. It's true, too. So many, many thousands haven't known Jesus, but He said, 'God so loved the world, that he gave his only begotten Son, that whosoever believeth on Him should not perish, but have everlasting life.' That *whosoever* means you, Merry, and me. And Jesus said another time, 'Him that cometh unto me, I will in no wise cast out.' "

"Eternal life doesn't interest me at all, Miss Ellen. I'm only interested in my baby and what I'll do all the years of my life after I have to give him away. I'll never be able to see a little child his age without wondering—"

"If it is God's will for you to have your child, you'll be able to have him. If you believe in Christ as His Son, if you take Him as your Saviour, nothing can and nothing will happen to you that is not for your good."

"But how do I do it? It would only be selfishness to take something for the good it would do me. Right now I'd do even that if I thought it would work. I don't know God or anything about Him, Miss Ellen. I can't imagine how anyone would love God or would want to. If there is a God, He's too far away. I've heard ministers say God is a kind heavenly Father. Well, if He's anything like my father, I can't imagine Him being kind."

"All fathers aren't what they should be, Merry, any more than all people are honest and fine. But God loves us. He made us and wants our love and trust. When we put ourselves completely in His care, we have peace and joy. Eternal life is important too; it means always and always and forever beyond time."

"I'm so tired, Miss Ellen, and I suppose I'm frightened too." Although the night was sultry, Merry made a little gesture of warming her hands around the steaming cup. "I just wish I could hold my breath and die. I wish I didn't have to live, but I'd be afraid to take my own life and I'm too determined to make my father suffer to muff the chance of putting myself out of the picture. Although," she laughed shakily, "maybe it would be the best way to hurt him. Think of the headlines." Now she gripped the spoon until it curled in her tight fingers. "If it weren't for my father, I could keep my baby. How I hate him. I would kill him if I could."

"Hurting your father won't help you, dear. He needs help and you may be the only one to give it to him."

"I wouldn't help him to save his miserable, selfish, proud life. Unless he changes his mind about my baby, I'll spend the rest of my life trying to ruin him."

"Your father has hurt Someone else much more than he has you, Merry, and that Someone died for your father as well as for you.

"No one has saved our lives; no one has died for us. I'm

sure I'd know it if he had. Oh, you are talking about—about—"
It was as if she could not say the name.

"Yes, I'm talking about Jesus. He didn't save your living
and breathing lives, Merry. The Lord died to save your souls,
and each wrong that you do or think and each right thing you
leave undone hurts Him."

Merry's laugh was one of scornful unbelief. "How could
God care about me, or how could He love anyone as mean as
my father?"

"When Jesus was dying on the cross, He prayed for the
men who put Him there. They were neither pleasant nor
kind."

"I wouldn't have done that. It just doesn't make sense,
Miss Ellen. Anyway, that was hundreds of years ago, and
my problem is in the present, not buried in the dead pages
of a book."

"Listen and *believe*, for it was written for you, too. 'As
many as received him, to them gave he power to become the
sons of God, even to them that believe on his name.'"

"But how, Miss Ellen? How?" For the first time in months
something sounded better than the thoughts of her own unhappy heart.

"How? Simply by realizing that you are a sinner in the
sight of God, that you know He will forgive those sins and
adopt you into His family when you accept Christ as your
Saviour. That means, Merry—" She paused to answer the
look of amazement and wonder on the girl's face. "That
means when Jesus died on Calvary's cross His shed blood
washed away all the sins of the people who had looked forward in faith to His coming and of all the people who would
live and believe on Him. People had believed since the garden of Eden that the Messiah would come. Here, listen."
The little nurse whipped out of her pocket her well-worn
Testament and began to read, " 'For God sent not his Son
into the world to condemn the world; but that the world

through him might be saved. He that believeth on him is not condemned: but he that believeth not is condemned already, because he hath not believed in the name of the only begotten Son of God. And this is the condemnation, that light is come into the world, and men loved darkness rather than light, because their deeds were evil.' "

"That's true." Merry nodded her head. "But I don't like to think of it that way. I want my world to be nice, but—it isn't."

"I know. Nothing is nice without the Saviour. Look at this, Merry. See, in I John 3:1 it says, 'Behold, what manner of love the Father hath bestowed upon us, that we should be called the sons of God.' "

"But how? I don't understand it and I—I want to. Suddenly I want to very, very much."

"Just believe, Merry. Would you like to pray, to ask Christ to come into your heart and be your Lord and Master?"

The girl was sobbing now. "I'm not worth it, Miss Ellen. But if He'll have me, if what you say is true—and I do believe it—I don't know why but all at once it is real. Yes. I do want to ask Him. O Lord, I'm sorry for my sins. I thank You for loving me even when I didn't know it. I don't understand fully about forgiveness and love, but I want to be different. I want You to be my Lord. I want to be like Aunt Margaret and Miss Ellen—and be happy. Please. Amen.

"I don't remember ever having a Bible read to me before, Miss Ellen, except when we went to see my grandmother when I was a small child. And I don't remember much about that. Could I read yours a little? Tomorrow I'll have Aunt Margaret pick one up for me."

"Take it, Merry, and keep it for your own."

"Thank you, no. I think this must be a very special book for you. I'll think of you using it with other people, other girls like me. Miss Ellen, is this why you stay here when I know you could make much more money someplace else? I heard Miss Anders tell Aunt Margaret a large hospital has offered you a very fine place."

"Shall we say a fine salary? There is no finer place than this. You see, the need is the same everywhere. Men and women, boys and girls, need to come to Jesus Christ."

Merry hurried to the empty sun-room and settled on a soft chaise lounge. Beginning with the very first gospel of John, she read it straight through. She stopped to ponder over Jesus' patience with the wise Nicodemus, of His compassion for the woman at the well; and she wept with Mary and Martha when she read of the death of their brother. When Merry read the words 'Jesus wept,' she sobbed softly and hugged the thought to her heart. He loved them! He cared for them and He cared for *her* too.

When she had finished, Merry knew that Jesus Christ was truly *her* Lord. There was a lightness in her heart she had never felt before, and somehow the heavy burden of the past few months had lifted. For the first time she could see the enormity of her own transgression. But He had died for her sin, and she knew the Lord wanted her to be happy and serve Him. It was almost confusing but infinitely comforting. Merry remembered her father, but the old feeling was gone. She could see even his mercilessness as different. Before, it had been an iron shaft aimed at her heart; now she recognized it as a death dart piercing his own soul. If she could only make him realize that! If Christ made that much difference in her life, and He had, He would help her talk with her father. Oh, it was wonderful to know the Lord! It had all come so suddenly—this release from hate and struggle.

She was sure that in some way her Saviour would help her no matter what the future had in store for her.

Merry had to tell someone that it was getting clearer, that all of her heart was different and happy. It was almost dawn and Miss Ellen was hurrying down the hall as Merry came out of the sun porch.

"It's all true, Miss Ellen, and it is better every moment. I want to read and read until I know all about Jesus. I'm so happy because I'm sure I belong to Him now."

There in the dimly lit hall, the little nurse raised shining eyes. "Thank You, dear Christ, for answered prayer," she said and then hugged Merry. "I'm so happy for you and for us all. Will you sleep now?"

"All day," the girl promised recklessly, but she knew she didn't want to sleep even if her eyes were heavy. She wanted to read and read until she could explain the miracle easily to others. She wanted to tell poor little Daisy that God loved her, too, and wanted her for His own.

6

New Life

MERRY DID SLEEP, but only briefly, and when morning came, she phoned Margaret. "Were you up, Aunt Margaret? Have you had breakfast yet?"

"Of course, my dear. Are you all right?"

"The most all right I've ever been. Oh, Aunt Margaret, I've found the Lord and He's so wonderful. Oh, He is wonderful!"

"Thank You, God. This is a happy day for me, Merry. I'll be over later. Thank you for calling."

But before Margaret arrived, Merry's small son took his place in the gleaming white nursery, and Merry lay quietly sleeping throughout the day.

Margaret waited under the cool oak trees and had a thanksgiving service all her own. When at length she was summoned to her niece's room, she entered quietly. "Are you all right, dear?"

"Of course, Aunt Margaret. Have you seen him? Have you seen my baby?"

"Yes, I've seen him and he's fine. Now, my precious child, I beg you for your own good, your own peace of mind, either keep this child, and I'll help you, or don't see him at all. Build your life on the wonderful promises you've accepted. Will you?"

"No. I can't promise that. I'll build my life on the wonderful promises I've just read about but I *must* see him." She

was so weary, Merry felt it hard to explain, but she had to—
to herself as well as to Margaret. "I'll build my life on the
new foundation because Jesus will be the center of everything I do and plan from now on. But I have to have my
baby as long as I can. I want to see him, Aunt Margaret. I
want to see him now."

See him she did, and from that moment Merry spent every
waking hour as near her child as she could. She hovered
over him when she was allowed in the nursery, bathed and
dressed him, took him out on the lovely lawn as soon as she
could and, from time to time, appeared completely absorbed
in the happiness of her new-found faith and the joy of loving
her child. By the change in her attitude, the smile always
on her lips, the serenity of her eyes, the people around her
knew that Merry was a new person.

Her mind was no longer focused only on her child and
their separation. Merry's kindness and deep concern for the
girls made her seek opportunities to talk with them. No one
used last names, and probably most did not use their own first
names, and none needed to tell her own story because essen-
tially each was the same as the next.

There was Sally, who kept her lips bright and her eye
shadow heavy. She had been there before and gave Beverly
Anders a bad time again. Unlike the other girls, she was
often defiant and rather brazen as she spoke of her "vacation"; but Merry found her one day on a bench at the far end
of their little park, her body racked with great sobs and her
breath coming fast.

"You need the same Friend I have," Merry said, sitting
down beside her.

Never had weeping stopped more suddenly. "I've seen
you smiling around the home. What do you have to be so
happy about?"

"I found out the Lord Jesus loves me and cares about me,"
she answered simply. "He loves you too."

"Yeah? It looks like it. Do you think I never heard of Christ?"

"I don't know."

"But you don't think I act like it?"

"No more than *I* did, Sally."

"Maybe for just as good a reason. Sure, I went to church and Sunday school too, until I went away to college and didn't have to. You know why I stopped?" She paused dramatically and spoke the next words with deadly fierceness. "Because there wasn't one thing real about anything I've ever heard. My mother held as many offices in her church service society as she did in her bridge club; my father was as occupied with church affairs as he was in the chamber of commerce and his own business because that assured him a better income. You know when I saw them? Usually on Sunday mornings in church. Sometimes at mealtimes."

"That's not what having Jesus as a Friend means, Sally."

"Sure, I know that too. What do you think I learned in Sunday school? Be kind to the mailman, the policeman and the janitor. Love all the people in the little old world; it's just a community, you know. Help get rid of slums and give the poor food to eat. And the same people who talked so big and taught so sweetly about the poor and being kind were nasty to salesgirls, cursed out repairmen, scolded their maids for nothing, were demanding of their children, and intolerant of anyone they didn't want to use. With religion, I've had it up to here." She drew a sharp hand across her throat.

"Oh, Sally, I didn't even have religion. That's not what I'm talking about anyway. I'm talking about the living Person, the Lord Jesus, who came to die for my sins and who rose from the dead and—"

"No Easter sermon for me. I'll never go in a church again—except for a wedding maybe. Won't I look just darling in white lace with six bridesmaids and candles and lilies? That's all my mother wants for me, and I may have it too."

"Just now you were weeping."

"Sure. Don't you ever get low? Cut it, Merry. You tried. Isn't that what you'll get a reward for? You don't have to win the sinner; you just have to make the effort."

Of course it wasn't true but Sally dashed off, giving Merry no chance to reply.

The next day Merry snatched a rare moment with Kit, the youngest girl in the home.

"Where are you going?" Merry asked as she caught up with her at the side door.

"I'm thinking of running away to join the hippies," Kit laughed, throwing back her head so that her long golden curls floated out behind her like angel's hair.

"What a life they must live!" Merry was searching for words.

"Not so bad, the way I see it. They do what they please; they make their own decisions. When they need to work, they do the least amount possible—and they must really live."

"What for?"

"For freedom, for one thing. I'm never going back home."

"Why not?"

"What's there to go back for? My parents were the best pals in the world, but now they're playing the heavy father-and-mother role. Mother was all for my dating the son of her best friend when we were just thirteen. We were the cutest steady pair! Then when she found this last spring that she had to send me away or cause a lot of talk, she collapsed. And my dad! Huh! If I told you the professions they're in, you'd flip. They flipped themselves and will probably never come out of it."

"They love you, I'm sure."

"You sound like some old social worker. Maybe they do. They've let me know in their nice, polite way that they'll really supervise me from now on. Not for me! You'll see my

picture in California when I leave here." She waved her
hand and fled around the side of the building.

There were some she did not even know other than by
sight. Pearl was older than most of the girls and beautiful
and very, very quiet. About her Merry could only wonder,
but she was sure Pearl was the girl her aunt meant when she
said later, "Sometimes Christians place themselves out of the
will of the Lord, and then their lives are off course until they
come back to Him."

Merry spoke often to Daisy and urged her to read the little
New Testament, but Daisy couldn't be bothered. She listened to Merry when she read, but she admitted, "It sounds
nice the way you say it, but me—I've got to have some fun."

The day was fast approaching when Merry's precious little
boy would go to belong to someone else. Margaret spoke of it
one morning. "I shall have to leave. My work is finished and
I've really overstayed my leave. Now I feel refreshed and I'm
going back with an urgency to dig deeper and deeper into the
problems of our district."

Merry said nothing but sat with her back straight against
the chair, her hands folded in her lap.

"Merry, you must go with me."

"I can't. You know I can't."

"My dear, the child will leave, too, unless you decide to
keep him."

The words were like a knife in Merry's heart. "Oh, no!"
The cry was wrung from her, and Merry's soft hands were
suddenly clenched tightly together. After a moment she
whispered, "I've known this must come, but I'm not ready.
I'll never be ready—nor willing. I think sometime—" Mar-
garet had said all she could say and the girl knew it. Finally
Merry asked too quietly, "Do you know where he's going?
Do you know who will have him?"

"Let me tell you simply this, my dear. These records are
never made public. Only the head of the institution is sup-

posed to know. The real parents, never—nor their relatives.
This much I can tell you. Your baby is going into a Christian
home, a home of comfort and security. I know. They don't
often tell us this much. Can't you be satisfied with this?"

"You know I can't, but it is better than nothing. How
much time do I have?"

"Until tomorrow."

"Oh no!" Again the sob was wrung from her. Merry left
the pleasant sun-room and fled to the far corner of the
grounds to a little clump of trees where she had often gone.
There she knelt in prayer, asking the Lord for strength and
another answer if He had it for her.

Before her child was born, it would have made no difference to know that he was going into a Christian home. Now
it made all the difference in the world. She was just as re-
luctant to give him up, but deep in her heart Merry realized
there was little she could do for him. She did not try to
keep back the tears as she tried to imagine the man and
woman who would become his father and mother. They
would have to want a child very much to take the baby of an
unknown. As Christians they would see him as a sacred
charge and a blessing—and a joy. They would love him, really
love him. He wouldn't be shunted off to exclusive camps and
schools just so his parents could be free of him.

Merry looked in her own heart and knew that keeping
down despair over not seeing him again would be a recurring
battle. She knew it would have been much easier and probably much more sensible if she had never looked at her child
nor held him in her arms, but she was not sorry she had gone
against Aunt Margaret's wishes.

She thought of Mike and wept again when she realized
she had been spared to know the Lord and he hadn't. They
had not questioned their right to love each other, for neither
of them had been troubled about a moral issue. To them the
words of a priest or justice of the peace could add only legali-

ty to their faithfulness to each other, and this they intended to have in their own time. Their love had been theirs alone and no affair of the rest of the world. Now Merry saw the difference. It was against God they had sinned; it was the Lord Jesus they had grieved. She thought of the religious training Mike had received, the catechism he had learned, and realized that what he had memorized had been words only. Had they meant anything to him, he would have talked with her about his faith and she would have listened. She would have respected anything Mike believed. She would have gone to church with him, but he had never asked her. He had only said they must be married in his church.

As for herself, Merry could see no excuse now. She knew, however, that Jesus had paid her debt and that, in the sight of God, she was "whiter than snow." Miss Ellen had shown her the verse—Psalm 51:7—and she believed it. Wishing and knowing now could not make things different.

Miss Ellen joined her there in the garden when her sobbing had stopped. There was peace in her soul, but she was glad for her coming. "Merry, there's a verse I want you to cling to and love and believe right now this very hour. It's Philippians 4:13: 'I can do all things through Christ which strengtheneth me.' My friend, you can do it. Now go in, have your dinner, pack your bag, and tell your baby good night. Then know that for you both there will be a glorious morning sometime in the Father's choosing when you will have eternity together."

The next morning when Merry, dressed in crisp, fashionable lines, stepped out of her room with her trim bag in hand, she knew before she looked that there would be only Daisy's tiny girl in the quiet nursery.

❀   ❀   ❀

They had driven briskly across the state, and, after a night in a comfortable motel and a breakfast of ham and biscuits and fruit, they were on their way once again.

Merry had said little that first day. Her eyes were often misty, but the tears didn't flow even when the two women were settled for the night. Margaret had driven with her lips tightly pressed together. She made little conversation, tried to get news on the radio, commented on the scenic beauty of the countryside.

They were still fifty miles from their destination when Merry broke the silence by saying softly, "I've decided what I want to do, Aunt Margaret, only I'm not just sure at this moment about the where. I want to go to some backward area and help people somewhat like Miss Ellen helped me. Not as a nurse but as a teacher."

"You mean a home missionary?"

"I suppose so. I'd like to be trained enough to sit by bedsides to do what a doctor orders without going into all of nursing. Mainly, I want to be able to talk to people and tell them about the lovely Lord. I've plenty of time for training."

"Are you sure, Merry? It sounds wonderful to me; and if that is the Lord's plan for you, there could be none better. Just be certain you aren't unduly influenced by a feeling of gratitude to Miss Ellen."

It was as though the girl had not heard. "I think I'd like to go away to school, but if being at home would help make it easier for Mums and Daddy to know Christ, I'll be glad to stay. I feel right now, without having seen them, that I should stay at home. At least I could help Marcia. What do you think?"

"I think you'll have to decide many things when you get home. Have you heard anything at all from them?"

"Nothing except the allowance that has been sent to you each month."

"That didn't come directly to me either. It was sent to my lawyer first, you know."

"We were both in hiding, Aunt Margaret. Didn't anyone know except your lawyer and Dr. Sam?"

"No one at all. Are you sure you don't want to go on to the apartment with me?" Margaret asked as she slowed down reluctantly before the huge house belonging to her brother.

"No. I'll be better off getting it over with all at once. What a strange way it is to come back to this old house, Aunt Margaret. It never was like a home, and now I feel as if I'd never been there except to peer through the windows."

"That is a bit true, isn't it, darling. But you aren't the same now."

Of course she wasn't. The strange thing was she wasn't just sure what she would be like in a few days. "That's growing," Margaret had explained when Merry told her that every day brought changes. Perhaps that was it.

But suddenly she was scarcely able to stand. Just less than two weeks since she first held that little boy in her arms and now—again she closed her mind to memories. But Merry knew it would be doubly hard to maintain a calm control, with her body still trembling from weakness, her faith so new and precious—and her loss a sharp pain within her.

"I've a long way to go," she sighed as she went up the front steps. "And there are three people who belong to me to whom I must show the way if it is God's will, and surely it is."

7

Strange Homecoming

MURPHY AND THE MAIDS greeted Merry with dutiful reserve but saw instantly there was something different about her.

"It's good to have you home, Miss Merry," the butler said, bowing as he took her bags.

"It's good to be back, Murphy." Surprisingly enough, it was true. "I hope you have all had a nice vacation with most of the family away. When is Mother expected back? Do you know?"

It was nothing unusual for this girl to ask information about her family of the servants. She had been doing it ever since she could remember. She had asked when she wanted to know, but she had rarely cared.

"Mrs. Johnson is expected back the first of next month with Miss Marcia. Your father will be home after dinner. He has dined at the club much of the winter and spring. Of course you knew he went over to France for a few weeks. Will you have dinner on the terrace, Miss Merry, or in the dining room?"

"On the terrace, thank you. And, Murphy, I wonder if Cook has any of her little rolls?"

"She made them special this morning, Miss. I'll tell her you asked."

"Do. Later I'll tell her I've been looking forward to them."

Her room was the same, except that gay garden flowers were on the tables and dresser, and the summer draperies were up. But the big canopy bed, the little Martha Washington chairs and her piano were all the same. Long after she had finished unpacking and putting away her clothes, Merry sat and played soft melodies and let her tears mingle with the plaintive music until she realized the servants would be waiting dinner for her. Cold water on her hot cheeks, a moment kneeling by her bed, and she slipped into one of last summer's evening gowns of russet sheer and floated down the deeply carpeted stairs, feeling much like a character in a play whom she might have to prompt at any moment. It had seemed foolish to dress for dinner when she would probably be dining alone; but never had Druscilla Johnson allowed informality after six, and Merry realized this point might antagonize her father if she did not conform. So she looked like a lovely pale princess with a touch of sadness about her as she stepped out on the terrace. No one would guess that she was a young woman whose heart was weeping for her lost child.

"You know, Murphy, it seems such a short time ago that I was playing ball there with Marcia, and you had to fish us both out of the lily pond."

"You did have a way of falling into water, Miss Merry. It caused us some anxious moments."

"You were always so kind to me, Murphy. I don't think I ever realized how good you and Cook were to me until this time while I was away with Aunt Margaret."

"Miss Margaret makes everyone look his best, Miss."

"More than that. She told me about Jesus."

"I was praying that she would, Miss Merry."

"But I wouldn't listen. One of her friends made me understand, though. Have you received the Lord, Murphy? Are you saved?"

"These forty years, Miss."

"I thought you must be. I remember how you used to try and tell Marcia and me about the Bible. But Daddy had told us not to listen; he said it was all nonsense. Please pray for me, Murphy. I'm going to try and talk to him about the Lord."

"I'll pray. Your father has a way of not seeing or hearing unless it suits his ideas. God alone will be able to speak to him, and we'll trust it will be through you."

There was much they did not need to say, Murphy and the girl. They both knew Margaret had loved and tried to help her brother; they both knew he had insulted her, avoided her and, in later years, had acted as though she no longer existed. Clark was a man marching toward a chosen destiny, sweeping aside everything that got in his way.

As she waited in the huge library, Merry fought her nervousness by wandering from one spot to another among the books, selecting a volume here and there at random, scanning first one and then another only to replace each on the shelves. "Precious little time I've spent in here," she murmured to herself.

It was ten o'clock before she heard the front door open and her father's brisk steps in the hall. Of course Murphy had phoned him of her return.

The girl went forward toward the half-open door, saying, "Hello, Daddy," with a soft smile and outstretched hands, which he chose to ignore.

"When did you get in?" was his reply.

"This afternoon around three. We had a beautiful drive, and Aunt Margaret sent her love."

"Humph. I'm glad you finished your classes, Merry. I didn't know you were enough of a student to do it by extension."

She laughed a gay little laugh, a new thing for Clark Johnson to hear. "Oh, I had a good governess."

"I expect you need some clothes. You'd better get busy

shopping and be ready, when your mother comes back, to go to Cape Cod for the rest of the summer. Then when fall comes, you can go on to college. I have it all planned out. You've really lost nothing." He spoke with a cold detachment he might have used to a groom about the care of a horse.

"I can't go back in the same way, Daddy. Not to the college we had talked about. All of my plans have changed since last month."

"Changed? How? They will change only if I think they should."

"I want to serve the Lord by helping people."

"More of Margaret's doing! What do you think it would look like for my daughter to be a religious fanatic? Don't you know I might be a candidate for governor this next election?"

"I should think that would look very well on your record, Daddy, if that's what's bothering you. I don't mean to argue, but I couldn't live the empty kind of life we have always had."

"Empty! You can't call our life that! You'll go to the college of my choice. During the Christmas holidays you'll make your debut as we have planned. Your mother has arranged for you to have the same date she made her debut, and has even engaged the same orchestra. We've already arranged it with the club, and the guest list was prepared a year ago. Two days before Christmas, we'll present our lovely daughter to our friends. Your mother is probably shopping for you in Paris right now."

"It never occurred to me that you were even considering a debut for me now. I'm so sorry I didn't know. I won't be here then; at least, I won't be free for the season."

"And why not? Haven't I had enough of this nonsense? You'll leave for school in September. You'll have the usual Christmas holidays, and even if you only had a few days, the studying you've done in the past few years doesn't indicate that you'd bring a box cf books home to spoil your vacation."

"I want to talk with you, Father. But—"

"I don't want to talk with you. Frankly, I don't look forward to another scene. But you seem different—as if you'd forgotten all about—that affair. I'm glad you've seen the light. But why this fuss over a debut? It is expected of you."

"I won't be having a debut, and indeed I have seen the light. I'm going to a Bible institute to prepare myself for work in some backward area. I don't know where."

Only once before had Merry seen her father completely lost for words, completely incapable of grasping an idea. After a moment he laughed the bitter, ridiculing laughter she had heard him use to make subordinates cringe. "You! Do mission work! What kind of work do you think a girl with your frivolous ways could do? They wouldn't even let you do maid work in a Bible school, let alone enroll in one. I thought you were different, Merry. I hardly thought you'd gone off the beam completely. You'd better run up the coast for the rest of the summer and get hold of yourself."

"I know it must seem strange." Somehow she was being given the strength to meet this moment. "We've never talked about these things, nor considered them important. But I've found Christ, and now I have the peace and joy only He can give. They *will* accept me in the institute."

"So you have found Christ!" The words came from his scornful lips with the sound of a curse. "I've heard such talk on street corners from those frights in black, but I never expected to see one of my own daughters 'get religion.'"

Merry smiled at him and, even in his anger, Clark Johnson could see in her eyes a new look, a new assurance that shook his skeptical soul. "You know, Daddy, we've never had anything real. Oh, we've had plenty of money and all the things it can buy. We've been able to go anyplace we wished and do all the things we wanted, but each new pleasure offered only a passing thrill; we were just as restless as before. A fleeting interest in *nothing* is what we've had most. We had nothing to cling to for time and eternity. Now, since I've known the Lord, I'm so happy to look forward to what He has planned for me. It is wonderful. I want you to know Him, too. May I tell—"

"Stop right there, Merry. My mother read the Bible, and read it to us children. There's nothing wrong with knowing what it says, but I'll tell you one thing, there's no one who can tell me he knows the Lord and have me believe him. Who can know God? And if one could, wouldn't you think He'd fix it so more could know Him instead of just a few fanatics?"

"Daddy, only listen." Merry hadn't lost her smile.

"To you? I suppose you think you have gone all out with this new idea. You are ready to believe you are going to heaven if you follow laws laid down by Moses, and going to hell if you fail to carry out the least commandment. Well, I'll tell you one thing, my girl. I'm having none of that here. You'll forget this whole mess or suffer the consequences!"

It was going no worse than Merry had expected. Now her prayers were to reach this man—this hardened sinner—with the words from God's own Book. "There's nothing I can do to win salvation, Daddy. I can only accept it. It is the free gift of God. Christ bought my freedom from sin and hell when He died on the cross. His blood washed me clean. 'But as many as received him, to them gave he power to become the sons of God, even to them that *believe* on his name.' Salvation is a gift, God's gift to us because He loves us, loved us enough to let His Son die on the cross. Oh, Daddy, won't you accept His gift now?"

The scowl on her father's face brought tears to Merry's eyes. "So you really believe that stuff? You really think you enjoy special favor with God? Let me tell you something, my saintly little daughter, no empty-headed harlot can teach me about life here or hereafter."

She shrank back from the words and fought back the flood of tears, but her voice was firm. "I'm only telling you what God has said. Not what I know of myself. Paul wrote, 'If any man be in Christ, he is a new creature: old things are passed away; behold, all things are become new.' Saul persecuted the church, but as the born-again Paul, he became the apostle to the Gentiles. Peter denied his Lord, but he repented. The woman at the well had a sinful past, but she believed and—"

"That will do, Merry. You may line yourself up with the repentant heroes of the past, but I've heard enough of this talk of sin and Christ. I've lived longer than you, with little cause for worry. I'll take my chances just the way I've always done. You get ready to go back to school—to the college we had planned for you—and forget this nonsense. Again, I suggest you begin by spending a day or two in town getting some new clothes."

"Thank you, Daddy, but I can't. I hate to argue with you. I don't want to be disobedient but I can't; I haven't the time. It really hurts me to go against your wishes because I want so much for you to understand. Can't you see? I can't live the old life anymore."

"Then you'll not live *any* life around here. You'll get out of this house until you follow the kind of life your mother and I have set up for you. This religious bug of yours need not ruin your whole life, nor ours. Your mother is happy to be coming home. She's had a hard time adjusting to everything and is just beginning to get on her feet—or she was when I flew over a couple of weeks ago. I'll not have her upset by a fanatic. Think it over, Merry. You'd have a rough time of it on your own. You won't be able to touch your uncle's money right away, you know. A few years without anything wouldn't be easy for a little spendthrift like you."

"When do you want me to go, Daddy?"

"You mean you'd actually defy me?"

"Not really. You're asking me to give up my Lord and His work. I can't go back to the parties we've always had. I can't dance half the night and spend the days dressing and shopping, and at the matinees. Cards and idleness would be impossible for me now. I love you but—"

"Where will you go? How will you live?"

"I don't know exactly, but the Lord will provide a way. I'm as sure of that as—"

"I've never seen Him do it. I don't want to see you turn into a beggar, but I suppose Margaret wouldn't let you do that. You'll find your allowance deposited to your account as usual. When you come to your senses, you may come home. Leave your address at the bank. I'll be in Chicago the rest of this week and your mother won't be back immediately, so take your time." He turned and walked from the room without even a backward glance.

When he slammed the door, the girl dropped to her knees. "O Lord, please bring him to You." She was shaking so much that she could only lean against the couch and quiet her aching heart by trying to recall that she was not alone—her new-found Saviour was with her. Her father had only berated her. The Lord had been beaten and crucified—for her and for her father. She struggled to a large chair and sat a few moments. Then she rang for Mrs. Murphy. "Will you help me pack, please. I'm going away soon and I think I'd like to go to Aunt Margaret's tonight."

"It's very late, Miss Merry."

"I know, but I haven't much to do. Do you think you could find someone who might want the things I leave in my closet? I'm going to a Bible institute this fall, and these would scarcely fit in with life there."

"If you give them to me before you leave, yes. We are always preparing a box for the missionaries."

"What a lot of fun they'd have just opening the box and seeing all the nonsense we'll put in. At least some would do for mosquito netting. Do you have a very large box, Mrs. Murphy?"

They began filling the box as soon as Merry called her aunt. "I've already started packing, Aunt Margaret. Now I'll ask; may I come?"

"You know you may. Shall I come over for you?"

"No, I'll bring my own car because I'll need it later, and I won't want to come back."

* * *

Margaret knew without being told that this young woman had endured almost more than she could bear. For a change, Margaret stayed in her city apartment the rest of the summer to keep Merry as occupied as she could.

A month later, Merry left the city for the Bible institute without calling or going to see the Bernardos. *I'll write to them when I am settled,* she told herself. *And when I come back for a visit I'll be able to go see them. Right now, I don't feel strong enough.*

8

Bible College

No AWKWARD COUNTRY GIRL ever felt more uncertain than Merry as she stood at last one September day at the door of the administration building. Here she would face very serious studying. Merry was amused within herself as she thought of the years she had spent in finishing school and the tremor she was feeling just now to face the registrar with whom she and her aunt had been corresponding.

It was surprisingly simple, this matriculation, and the Merry who stood in line with her finished papers and wrote her name and signed up for classes looked very young and delighted.

In no way did she sense she was any different from the others, but they felt it and loved her for the eagerness with which she attacked each serious task. To Merry, the girl who had only recently learned to make a bed and do her own laundry, this struggle of getting a room in order, hanging up clothes, going down the hall to wash and iron her dresses, was a great adventure.

In spite of her concentrated reading of the summer, she was almost too terrified to enter a classroom with young people who had been brought up in Sunday school and church. So, for the most part, Merry had no idle moments. She pored over her books; she almost memorized her notes;

she haunted the library and ended by spending much of her generous allowance on any book the professors casually mentioned in class.

"These should make our study much easier, Sue," she said to her auburn-haired roommate as she began to unpack a large box. "Maybe they'll help us both. At least I hope there is something in here you can use too, even if you are a senior."

Susan Perry dropped on her bed beside Merry, kicked off her slippers and tucked her tiny feet under her as she propped herself against the pillows. "To think I had to wait two whole years for a roommate like you. Can you tell me why you didn't order a larger library instead of just a few books?"

"Have I done something—strange?"

"Something strange, she asks. Sweetie, some of us might have gathered together a few of those books, but only the fellows who dig in and have real bang-up jobs are able to start out as graduates with something like you had delivered to our door today."

"Oh!" Merry looked blankly at her and then began to laugh. "I've a lot to learn. Perhaps I just haven't the time to take things too slowly."

"If you plan to learn all that this first year," Sue said, sweeping her hand over the boxes yet unpacked, "this old building has served its purpose. You'll be the new dean or instructor general. What are you taking anyway?"

"The dean helped me, so I suppose the schedule is all right. Old Testament survey, history, English, introduction to religious education, organ and freshman missions. Does that sound all right to you?"

"Yep. Now let's go to the lounge. One of my jobs as your big sister and roommate is to help you get oriented. It's going to be a pleasure, and soon out of my hands, unless I miss my guess."

"That's lovely of you, but no thank you, Sue. I'd like to start that another day. I've some reading to do."

"Look, sweetie, you don't have to finish the first semester tonight or even this week. You've got to get oriented outside of classroom, too. How can I play the big sister if you're planning to stay in our room all the time? Don't look so worried. It won't hurt you. Coming?"

"I'm not exactly worried, Sue. And thank you. I keep saying that, but I do mean it. I guess I'm a little tired and a little anxious to study. You'll forgive me this time. I'll turn in early and perhaps another night—"

Later in the week Sue tried again and wasn't sure what was said or how her young roommate managed it, but she, the senior girl, was on her way down the stairs alone feeling a bit confused. When she went back later, Merry was asleep with her book tucked under her cheek.

So it continued. Thanksgiving came and Merry departed in a cab for the airport to meet Margaret and spend the holidays with her in a downtown hotel. Sunday night they both came back to the campus, and Margaret wandered around for four days like a nostalgic alumna until the dean of women approached her with the question "Would you like to stay and teach a class, Margaret?"

"Does it show that badly? I'd love to stay. Frankly, I'd like nothing better than to listen in at one of your conferences with the girls; I'd like to watch you when you are really in harness."

"It *would* be cheating, Margaret, but I understand what you mean. Sometimes I get so bogged down with all the activities, I long to see how someone else does it! Doesn't it seem a long, long road we've traveled since the day we entered our first year of college?"

"Yes. And you were always *so* intellectual, Hester. How did you manage all you did?"

"Only did what I wanted, then as now. You know that. And who's talking about IQs? You were in every honor society."

"How is she doing, Hester? My Merry, I mean."

"I'm afraid the child will be the top student in her class. She's working harder than any other girl we have, but she's not having much fun."

"I'm afraid she doesn't know how."

"What is it, Margaret? What makes her so intense?"

"Many things, probably. She's young and very serious. Weren't you like that?"

"Never, and you know it. She hasn't even gone out on one date."

Even to her old friend, there was much Margaret would not disclose. It would do no good. It was not necessary, but what she could tell, she did.

"She's had dates enough for a good long time. Remember, Hester, she wasn't looking for even a little pleasure when she came here. She thought she had had all of that she'd ever want in her life. This school itself is much more exciting to her than it could possibly have been to us. We had Christian parents; we can't remember a time when we hadn't heard about the Lord. To Merry all of this is completely new." Was this adequate? Margaret thought so; she could not tell her friend that Merry carried a heartache she could neither share nor forget.

Shortly before Christmas, Merry opened a letter, gave a little squeal, hugged Sue and twirled around their little room. "Aunt Margaret wants you to come home with me for Christmas. It will be simply wonderful to have you there. You'll love her and—"

"Honey, don't you know?"

"Know what?"

"I have to stay here throughout this holiday. Oh, I don't mind, because it is the only way I can finish the semester. I'm to relieve Ruth at the switchboard and that will give me the board money I need. In addition to that, I've planned some parties and a play for my Sunday school class. The details are just about all worked out; I knew I'd stay on here."

"Oh, Sue, that doesn't seem fair. I thought you were staying just because your family is all the way up in Alaska. Isn't there anyone else who can keep the switchboard? Couldn't you make it up another time?"

"I'm afraid not, Merry. And I really don't mind. I'm just so happy to have this opportunity to make enough to keep little ol' Sue in bread and potatoes. Don't I look like I need it?" She laughed and picked up her notebook.

"Oh, I didn't realize. I'm so sorry."

"Why should you be? I'm not. I'm having a beautiful time and Christmas here can be just as lovely as any place in the whole world because the Lord is here, too. We'll have a tree and Mother wrote that they'll call me any time that day that I can be free. Don't you know I'll be right on top of that phone the minute we set?"

This was new to Merry—new and troublesome. She had known there were real needs in the world, and she knew some of the girls at the school had jobs; but she hadn't realized so completely before that their working was essential to their staying in school. From then on she began to watch —furtively, of course, but very carefully.

In spite of all the books she had bought, she had spent so little of her allowance the balance in the bank was much higher than it had ever been in her life. She looked at her checkbook in surprise. She had not even been aware of the amount, only that it was sizable. Now she took an afternoon that was free, went to town, cashed a large check, addressed half a dozen envelopes and stuffed them.

The first to be mailed was not to Sue but to Patty, the girl down the hall whom Merry had heard talking over the nightly laundry.

"I'm not worried," Patty had said. "I knew that secretarial job wouldn't last very long, and I'll get another job. I always do. You know this is the type of thing that tries our faith. I'm just going to trust."

So Patty's words as well as Sue's were very much in her mind as Merry filled her envelopes and went back to the dorm. In her own room, she showed her new shoes to Sue and knew they could explain her long absence. "They aren't exactly what I wanted," she said, "but they are serviceable. The snow has been deeper than I expected so I got boots to go over them. Higher boots than the ones I thought I'd need here."

"Didn't you have high boots last year?"

"Yes, but I left them at Aunt Margaret's. It's such a nuisance moving so many things. These I can leave here over the summer, if I pass. Oh, Sue! When will I ever learn? One pair of boots is enough for one girl. Your eyes said it. I'll stop being a spendthrift."

Suddenly there was a catch in Merry's throat. That was what her father had called her. A spendthrift. In a way she was. She certainly had been. But she'd never spend in the same way, she was promising the Lord in her heart. No. I'll spend for you, dear Lord, and I'll spend it as fast as I get it.

As she picked up her mail the next day, Patty asked for hers. When the girl opened that certain envelope, she actually turned pale. "Look, Miss Hester." She turned to the dean who was standing near. "There must be some mistake. This couldn't be for me."

"Let me see, my dear. No, there doesn't seem to be a mistake. Isn't there a note inside?"

"Not even a scratch on the paper. No, just my address on the outside with my name. I don't *know* anyone who could send money like that to me or anyone else. Miss Hester," she continued, her voice trembling with excitement and emotion, "this means I can finish out this year without putting Dad in a hard place. You know a job just hasn't turned up.

Perhaps when I get one I can even write and tell him not to send me any more. But how would anyone know I was down to my last thirty-two cents? See, the postmark says it is from the city."

When four more girls received similar envelopes, Hester Smith might have guessed, but she said nothing.

Sue had her envelope after a long afternoon at the nearby city mission. She didn't even open it until she reached her room, dropped her books on the desk and had hung up her coat. "A letter from Mom and Dad," she said and read it with tantalizing slowness. "They are making all kinds of plans for next year when I'll be with them, Merry. I can scarcely wait. I've loved every minute of being here in school, but Alaska has always been home to me. Come along with me this summer, Merry, and see it for yourself."

"We might drive up there someday, Aunt Margaret and I. It would be fun if we could find a good excuse." Merry watched as her roommate tore open *the* envelope.

"I don't believe it!" Sue gasped. "Merry, is this real? Can you see it too?"

"What, Sue?"

"This plain little ol' fifty-dollar bill, silly."

"It's right there in your hands."

"Merry, it is just like it was for some of the other girls. Did you know Patty got one too? And she doesn't even know anyone in this area, except at school. Do you think someone is having them mailed here just to throw us off? I don't deserve this. I can get by. But think of the riches of it." She hugged her knees and tossed the bill on the desk. Then she fell back on the bed in a mock faint. "Am I awake?" she asked.

"Of course you're awake. Get up or you won't be."

Sue slipped to her knees beside her bed and, although her prayer was a silent one, Merry knelt at her own bedside and rejoiced in her new-found field of service. Quietly she prayed, *Thank You, Lord, for giving me an opportunity to serve You this way. Make me a good steward for Thee. In Jesus' name. Amen.*

✿   ✿   ✿

"Merry, go shopping with me," Sue asked early the next Saturday morning while they were putting their room in order for the day.

"When? I love to shop."

Never had Merry liked it so much nor had she ever had such an experience. Sue took her downtown to a street away from the main shops and, with long-time experience, slipped in and out of little stores. Although she spent less than Merry usually did on one dress, the senior girl was radiant with her purchases, and loaded with parcels.

"See, I thought I could get what I needed with twenty dollars. I've got six cents of that left. Now I can give my class a real Christmas party and send some home for Mom to use on Eskimo presents. Hurry, or we'll miss dinner at the dorm."

Christmas came and Merry sent gifts and a loving note to her mother, her father and Marcia, but heard nothing in reply. There were moments when she thought her heart would burst with joy at this her first Christmas as a Christian—or with sorrow at this her first Christmas bereaved by her own hands.

Midterm came and went, and she thought she would faint at the first exam. But it wasn't nearly as bad as she had expected. Merry said as much to Sue when the lights were out and they were almost asleep. "It was actually about the things I've been reading."

"What did you think they'd test you on, Merry? Relativity? It's an old institute custom to give exams on the subjects you've been taking."

"That was stupid, wasn't it? Oh, Sue, this is a wonderful place. Don't you hate to think of leaving in June?"

"In a way I do." There was something in the senior's voice that revealed much more than Merry could understand at that moment.

9

Jack

BRUCE MACALLASTER had walked with Merry across the campus; he had found a place beside her during the long study hours in the library; and twice she had gone with him for cokes when the library closed at nine. She had no excuse not to when he said so matter-of-factly, "You'll stop for a sandwich with me tonight."

He was comfortable to have near. His slight Scotch burr was pleasant to her ears and his thoughtful attentions a solace when her books became confusing and her spirits lagged, as they sometimes did.

However, Merry did not see him as an attractive young man in whom she might become interested, but only as a symbol of a young Christian studying to learn how to tell sick humanity about the great physician. Somehow he sensed her need for understanding silence as well as for long serious talks.

Other men looked at the beauty of Merry's face, the aesthetic remoteness of her eyes, the sweet seriousness of her mouth, and tried to make friends, to talk with her, to take her to concerts or to study groups, but she did not see them. She said no without seeming to know she had spoken—or worse still, without even being aware she had been spoken

They talked of her among themselves and wondered, because no other girl in the school was like her. The others took time to wander in the parks, to visit the shops, to chatter in the lounge. They enjoyed their dates and were obviously delighted at the attention of the men students. What was more natural than that a minister would like to choose a wife who was well trained in the work for the Lord? Already there were a dozen couples who were sure that God had let them meet for His own glory and their happiness. Of course Merry saw the fun and fulfillment around her, and she was well aware of the burst of early spring in hearts if not in atmosphere. But she connected none of this with her own life.

Jack Evans took her problem more seriously than some of the other young men because he could picture Merry, and no other, pouring his coffee and sitting beside his chair all his life long while he prepared sermons and planned his work.

He watched Bruce and tried his methods, but Merry didn't know it. She loaned him pencils, talked over different passages, smiled and thanked him when he carried her books; and—when he asked her to go out with him—said no with a faraway look in her eyes.

One late March day when the world was wrapped in white, he burst out at Bruce as they met on the campus, "What goes? Is she in love with you? Why can't she even see me?"

"You mean Merry?"

"Of course I mean Merry. I'd give ten years of my life if she'd marry me. I can't even get her to walk to the bookstore with me unless I meet her 'accidentally.' She treats me like a friendly puppy."

"I don't know why. There is more seriousness about her than any other girl I ever saw, and more sweet beauty except in one."

"Aren't you in love with her, Bruce?"

"No, Jack. Perhaps I would be if there weren't a girl in Canada waiting for me."

"Does Merry know?"

"Of course, and Bess has written to her. Perhaps that's why she lets me walk with her."

"You mean she isn't interested in love? She doesn't want marriage? She's too young, too lovely, to lead a cloistered life."

"Speak to her. Let her answer your questions. I'm only her friend."

"Then give me a chance, Bruce. Stop monopolizing the girl."

"I didn't realize I was, Jack. At times I'm lonely for Bess, and I know Merry has a loneliness too. I'll pray for your happiness."

Part of the answer Bruce knew, part he thought he guessed. He knew she came from a family of great wealth, great opportunity, and the burden of the unsaved parents and sister lay heavy on her heart. He had never questioned Merry, nor did he intend to now.

However, Jack did. He met her in the hall the next morning when the sun was making a blinding light of the deep hard-crusted snow.

"I've some calls to make in my parish. Come for the rest of the day with me, Merry. I know your classes are over."

"Your parish?"

"I have a small country church twenty miles out of town. Because it is so near I can do a lot of things the other fellows can't with theirs. So I take this day about twice a month to visit. Come with me."

"I can't, Jack. Thank you for asking me."

"Why can't you?" There was hurt as well as anger in his eyes. "Why do you say no every time I speak to you? Why? Am I repulsive to you? Or do you think yourself above the common herd?" When he saw the quick tears that covered her pale face and the shock in her eyes, Jack was instantly contrite. "Oh, Merry, forgive me. Whatever it is, let it go. Just don't look like that."

Still she stood there, too shocked as yet to find the right words.

There in the alcove by the window, he dabbed at the tears on her cheeks and tried to undo the hurt.

Finally she reached out and took his handkerchief to brush away the tears. Then Merry answered shakily, "You are anything but repulsive, Jack. I can only ask you to forgive me if I've been unkind; I didn't mean to be. I don't think I realized that I haven't been a part of the normal school life, but suddenly I can see many things." She laid her hand on his arm in a gesture of remorse and friendship. "I'm really sorry. I'd like to go for a day with you." When she saw how happy her decision made the man in front of her, tears came to her eyes again, but not with such force. "Perhaps I can explain why I acted—strangely."

"Just go with me. I won't care why you haven't gone before. Or what you've done."

Merry gave him a startled look, then realized he was only referring to her withdrawn indifference at school.

Later as they rode over roads, snow-cleared and smooth, she tried to explain a little about her attitude. "You see, Jack, I've only known about Jesus less than a year—just since last July. Sometimes my sister and I were sent to Sunday school; usually though we went to church only at Christmas and Easter. Then we were beautifully dressed and terribly excited about the presents and parties that were always a part of the holiday seasons. The dances were the greatest events, especially during Christmas week. If we were exposed to a gospel message, I didn't hear it; few did. Then this summer a lovely young woman told me about the Lord. I read the gospel of John straight through and the Lord really spoke to my heart. I've known ever since that He has something special for me to do." Merry paused briefly because it was the first time she had spoken of these things to anyone her own age except Sue. She had talked with the president of the school and the dean of women, of course. Now she continued a bit breathlessly, "That gospel of John was the first scripture I had read. Now I know I've so much to read, so much to learn, that I've been trying to crowd it all in at once. Maybe I've been rude."

"You've been very lovely," Jack assured her. "We all thought you were too dedicated ever to have known anything but a life set almost apart as a convent existence."

Merry laughed. "Just the opposite. I'll be more friendly. Why, Jack, I believe I've been missing people. I mean people for their own sakes. Christian education isn't all work, is it?"

"No, you have to start teaching a Sunday school class next term, and surely you'd find it out the hardest way if you didn't before then."

Merry laughed again. "I'll have a lot of catching up to do. I'll write a motto and put it on my mirror—a motto Aunt Margaret's housekeeper gave me in a letter last week. It said, 'A lady never seems to think of herself at all.' That's why Miss Margaret makes people comfortable just to be near her."

"Why would she give *you* that motto?"

"When I was home at Christmastime we were talking about character building. Becky could easily teach a class in psychology although she'd not use a textbook nor the words of one."

"She sounds like an interesting person herself."

"Becky is. She's simply wonderful." Then Merry launched into tales of Becky and Horace, Aunt Margaret and Dr. Sam. "I've talked too much," she said as they turned off the main highway. "Tell me what you want to do, Jack."

"Because I feel the pull of the work so strongly, I'm glad this is my last year here. I want to go to an almost forgotten

people, the Indians of Guatemala, as a missionary. I know
there are missions among them but I want to go deep into
the jungles with radio, records and Bibles. I want to live
among them and be their friend. It's the only way, of course,
and nothing new or untried; but it hasn't been tried enough.
Well, here we are. Mind cuddling under this blanket while
I run into the general store to make a phone call?"

Merry pulled a small book out of her purse but could not
become absorbed. It was fun to sit there and watch the door
as people moved in and out, their eyes squinting in the glare
of the sun on frozen snow.

"It's all right. I knew it would be. The Ecklars were expecting me to have the noon meal with them. They are now
expecting us both."

"Are they special?"

"Very. They've been my good friends as well as church
leaders. I can talk to them."

Soon they drove into a large yard where the deep snow
covered the beautiful bushes around a neat brick house.

"Just what will we do here?" Merry asked, uncertain of
her new role.

"We'll visit, talk over church affairs, have dinner and go
on to three or four other homes for short visits. I'll have you
back at the dorm by six o'clock."

The huge fire in the old brick fireplace was no less warming than their hostess' greeting.

"I'm so glad you've come, Merry. I've wanted Jack to bring
his girl for a long, long time now."

Merry gave her gay little laugh. "I'm afraid you'll be disappointed then, because I'm just a friend, but I hope a very
special one."

Jack's eyes were serious as he took her coat, "Katy Ecklar,
you're too impulsive. Of course she's the girl I want to be
my girl, but give me a chance to tell her myself."

"Well, of course. Now that you have, come into the kitchen while I finish my cake." She led them through a charming dining room with urns of begonias filling the windows and on into the kitchen, spicy with the heady odor of red geraniums on the sill.

"I'm to learn more about cooking this summer during vacation," Merry confided. "Becky has promised to teach me."

"Didn't you learn to cook in high school?"

"Oh, no. I suppose I didn't learn much that was useful."

"I'll teach you," Jack offered. "I can cook beautifully. I was a Boy Scout."

"I'll need to know a lot about cooking. I'm training for Christian guidance for the home mission field."

"Not if I can help it," Jack said, then turned to their hostess. "I'm going to put on my boots and meet Paul in the field."

When he had gone out the door, the pretty young housewife turned to her guest. "He's serious, Merry. Don't hurt him."

"How can I? This is the first time I've been out with Jack."

"But not the first time he's wanted you to go out with him. I probably shouldn't say it, but the week after you came to school, he told us he had seen the girl he wants to marry."

The tears in Merry's eyes and the quiver in her voice were more convincing than her words. "You'll have to help me persuade him to think of someone else. Please."

"Why? Don't you like him?"

"Of course. How could I help it?" Merry could not tell her that she had a heartache she could not share with anyone. She could not tell of her great longing to help girls such as Daisy whom she had known in the house that to her was a place of sorrow, a house of parting. "There is no place in my life for love and marriage now. There may never be. I've so much to learn and so little time to give to anyone as yet. I'd be his greatest liability."

"You really mean that, don't you? You are terribly serious."

"Oh, yes."

"I don't know why but I believe you are right. Don't you think, though, after a few years—"

"I don't. I don't think I'll ever—"

Then the door burst open and the men came in. Mrs. Ecklar gave Merry a reassuring pat and, after the introductions, sent the men into the living room while she and Merry finished the dinner preparations.

It was a gay meal with talk of the church, of the Sunday school program, and of the youth work which they planned to expand in the summer.

"In a few months the church will be ready for a full-time pastor," Jack said over his bowl of homemade ice cream.

"Will you stay, Jack?" Mr. Ecklar asked. "We'd like to have you permanently. This isn't official, but we've been talking it over. We want you to be our regular pastor."

"I'd like that too, Paul, but I feel compelled to go south to my Indians. If I could be two places at once—but you know where my heart is leading me. I should say where I feel the Lord has been directing me all along."

"When will you know?"

"Any time now. The details aren't final but in my own heart I'm positive of the answer."

"Yes, you could be."

By two-thirty Jack and Merry were on the circuit, stopping at first one home and then another for a few minutes of good conversation over hot tea and cookies or steaming coffee and cake.

"I like them all," Merry said as they sped through the early darkness made denser by a new flurry of great snowflakes. "But most of all, I like Katy Ecklar."

"They like you too. It's easy to see. You'll go with me again." It was more of a statement than an invitation.

"Probably not!"

"Why, Merry? What have I done?"

"It's not you. It's just that I can't spend your time so light-ly. You need a lovely wife to share your days in Guatemala." She was half laughing, half teasing. "You would only waste your time with me. I've a project of my own I think the Lord would have me develop. So far, I can't talk much about it because I'm not sure of the why or how."

"Why *not* Guatemala?"

"No, Jack. Whatever I'm to do, I'll do it alone. At least for a long, long time."

"Is there someone else, Merry? That's all that would make me give up and, at that, not until I see a gold band on the proper finger."

"Talking won't help, Jack. It certainly won't help me. Perhaps I was wrong to come today."

"No, not wrong. But after today, do you think I'll be satisfied with anything less?"

"You'll have much, much more. Surely you will."

"What are you waiting for, Merry?"

"I know about some of the waiting, Jack. But mostly I just know that I must. Men aren't the only ones with convictions."

His reply was a grim "No, but I'll ask you again."

Merry decided she'd try not to give him the chance.

10

Sue's Secret

"Where have you been?" Sue twirled around from the desk in mock disapproval. "Really, Merry, for a girl who never leaves the dorm for more than an hour at a time, for a girl who studies from three until midnight six days a week, for a girl whose habits are like a map, you certainly had me worried."

"Oh, I've just been finding out today I've been a complete idiot. Everyone must think I'm too odd to live. Believe it or not, I had a nice time away from the library, away from school."

"Miracle. What did you do? I thought you had gone AWOL."

"I left a note for Miss Smith."

"You don't think I'd ask her, do you? Then you would have been in trouble."

"Silly, I'd ask her anything. So would you. Why so much concern?"

Suddenly Sue paused and almost whispered, "What *has* happened to you, Merry? You look different—radiant."

"I think something has. I was lost in a great dark forest. It was a beautiful forest, Sue, and I knew the Lord was with me, but there were no people. I had a lovely time but I was almost alone. Only today was I led out." She grabbed Sue's hands and whirled her around in a mad spin. "It's a wonderful world, Sue, and people are lovely. Let's go call on all the dorm."

In a rush Sue swept her roommate to a chair, felt her forehead and reached for her wrist. "Nope, not even racing—unless—Merry, are you in love?"

"I thought I told you. I'm in love with the whole human race."

"Couldn't be just that! This is the first time you've seemed like—"

"A part of the human race?"

"No, a very young, happy girl!"

"Thank you. It's the first time I've felt like one for a long, long time."

"Were you alone today?"

"No, Sue. I rode out to his parish with Jack Evans."

"You could call him the whole human race and I wouldn't disagree."

"Sue, do you like him?"

"Like him? Who wouldn't?"

"Oh, darling, precious, remarkable Sue. You do, and you will more and more. And will you—I don't know what—but act like it?"

"Why? Why? Didn't you have a nice time? Don't you want to—to—"

"Oh, Sue. No. He's wonderful, but not for me. He needs a girl like you."

"Of course he does, but how'll he find that out? Merry, I don't understand but I'm all for it. Didn't you know? He's the only fellow I've *seen* since I've been here in school, and he's only taken me out for coffee or the concerts a few times, but not at all this year. That was all the first two years. He's polite this year, but he's scarcely glanced at a girl."

Merry laughed softly. "This is the first time I've seen you flustered."

"But, Merry, did he ask you for another date?"

"Yes, but I can't go."

"Busy?"

"No."

"Then why?"

"It's one of those 'just because' things."

"Don't you like him?"

"I love him, but he's not for me," she insisted.

"You said you'd be busy. How can you explain that to a man who wants to date you and you want to say no? How can you know you are going to be busy?"

"I'm going to get acquainted with the maids and men. I'm going to get oriented like you thought I should months ago. Isn't it about time?"

"Sweetie, all you need do is smile. Everyone knows you by now; they will like it if you find out who is walking down the hall with you and sitting by you in class or at meals. But I'll never understand it."

She could not know that Merry had set herself apart for work. She longed for the time when she could go out into the city mission and put into practice the facts she had been learning. *Girls mostly, dear Lord,* she prayed again that night. *Use me to talk to them about Jesus. Help me to make them understand He is all in all, that even if they have no love in their homes, Christ can supply everything. O God, may my suffering make me able to help someone else.* Then, hastily, as if the Lord could not know her own loving heart, she prayed with tears blinding her eyes. *Dear Lord, I do have joy in Thee. I'm so grateful that I know Thee, but the sadness comes when I think of that little boy somewhere. And I wonder, dear Lord, how I wonder—* Merry knew it wasn't necessary to go on. Besides, how could she? She pondered and she thought. Somewhere he was learning to walk, perhaps he was talking. Perhaps—perhaps.

It was at moments like these that she snatched her little

Testament and sped across the campus toward the chapel, re-peating over and over whole chapters until her heart was calm and she could again join the young people in the lounge or the dining hall or as they studied in the library.

So it was one day when Jack was on his way to the dorm to try to persuade Merry to go to the mission with him that night. He saw her open the door and dash down another walk as if all the powers of darkness were pursuing her.

Jack knew she didn't see him, as he hurried after her and finally caught up, he heard Merry sob, "Blessed be the name—"

"Merry, is something wrong? Has something happened?"

Even as she turned, the tears were brushed away. "Oh, Jack. Sometimes—sometimes I get in my own way, or rather, in the Lord's way for me. I've heard chopping wood is good, but there aren't old stoves around to warm us, so I substitute a run on the campus for wood chopping and a session in the chapel for violent exercise."

"May I run with you?"

"No, I'm all right now."

"Well, it's a good idea. Let's run about twenty blocks to the mission; that's my assignment for the night. Old Bruce picked up a virus and is laid low. Come along, Merry. Come with me and sing for us, please."

"No can do. I'd trip over the chairs and fall flat in the aisle from fright. Oh, don't say it. I'll get over that, but not tonight."

Jack couldn't figure out how she did it, but by seven o'clock his plans were completely changed and, instead of Merry, it was her roommate who played for the meeting and later sang the song he had wanted Merry to sing.

"Beats me, Bruce," he said later after he had reported about the meeting. "Merry will hypnotize the heathen, mes-merize any mission she goes to. I had no more intention of taking anyone else than the man in the moon. Sue's a good girl, though, and she plays and sings well."

"She's pretty too," Bruce added. "You could go a long way and do worse."

"Cut it, Bruce. I'm not shopping. I found what I wanted at first glance. I'm not looking any farther."

"She may be though, old man. I don't know why, but Merry impresses me as a strong-minded little gal."

Across the campus the conversation in the girls' room was somewhat different. "I don't know why *you* shouldn't go with him," Sue said as she brushed her hair. "He's—" She paused for the right word, then added very primly, "very nice."

"Oh, Sue. He's wonderful and you know it, but he doesn't, which makes him all the nicer. Good night. I'm glad. I'm glad of many things. Now let's get some sleep."

That summer Merry didn't go to the seaside to spend the hot months with Margaret; instead, she insisted on taking both terms of summer school in order to finish in a shorter time. Sue went back to Alaska only for a month. After that she and Jack spent their honeymoon on their way to *their* mission field in Guatemala.

11

Merry's Goal

"I'M NOT AT ALL TIRED," Merry insisted when fall came and the new school year started. Perhaps she wasn't. She sped through the campus on winged feet. She rushed from classes to study groups, to work in the community house, to take her class of girls on sightseeing trips in the city, to take them in her car away from the busy town to a country spot where they could see actual cows and horses, pigs and chickens. She went to concerts and took turns at the desk if anyone asked her.

The dean called her in after midterm exams to talk a long hour. "Merry, is your schedule too heavy?"

"Oh, Miss Smith, have I flunked?"

"Scarcely that. You always seem in such a hurry. We are concerned lest you wear yourself out. You are doing twice as much as the girls who are working their way through school."

"It's just—just that—oh, there's so much to do and so little time."

"My dear, I've thought that all my life, and every year I'm more convinced it can't all be finished in three hundred and sixty-five days or even more."

"No." There was teasing in Merry's tone. "But Miss Smith, we all think you try."

"Touché. I may deserve that! You've done unusually well

this session, Merry. What are your plans for the summer? Would you like to be a counselor in a Christian camp?"

"Not this summer. I want to stay here and go both terms again. If I do I can finish in January of next year. Then I can begin real work."

"Where, Merry? Would you like to stay here in the city? The director of the community house asked me if she can keep you this summer to start you toward full-time work when you finish."

"I've been thinking of that, Miss Hester. Between summer school and the regular school year, Aunt Margaret and I ran away to the hills of West Virginia. Once when I was a child we had gone on a vacation to White Sulphur Springs, but we didn't stop there this time. We went exploring deep, deep into the hills. I loved it and the people there. Do you think there would be a place for me somewhere in our Southern mountains?"

"There are places crying for workers, Merry. Mostly the problem is to find the money to support them. But God will provide the place you are needed, my dear, and the means to keep you there as well."

"Miss Hester, this time we'll just ask the Lord to provide the place. Long ago He provided the means when a great-uncle set up a trust fund for me. Will you help me pray for the place?"

"Of course, and next year when you come back in September, there will be a list of places. There is always a list. Then we will ask God definitely to show us His choice."

❖ ❖ ❖

"I like it all," Merry wrote to Margaret when September of the final year came. "All except the jail services, and I keep telling myself that should be the easiest of all because they can't leave. But really, Aunt Margaret, the faces of the women are so miserable, so unhappy and bitter. There's one woman who looks like she's seventy. When I tried to talk with her after the service, she spoke in a soft, almost youthful voice. The matron told me she's a regular. She's done almost everything and looks it. Poor thing is still in her forties, but her lined face, dirty gray hair, and hands that shake constantly make her pathetic. Sometimes she seems to listen; usually she just sits and scowls. Then there are the young girls, frightened and brazen by turn. They'll listen, ask questions and sometimes respond. Three accepted the Lord last week, and I know it was real for each of them. They will be paroled in the care of Christians, and there's where the big job begins.

"I like best the children's classes where their little hearts are open and their prejudices aren't established. You know how eagerly they seek the beautiful. One little boy said, 'If Jesus were to come to my house, He would make it all shiny and bright.' I know why that was important to him because I was there calling several weeks ago. It was the first time I had ever been in an inner apartment that had windows opening only into two rooms, the front and the back. The apartment was clean and well kept, but it was dark. Most of them are filthy hovels. Still the children are seeking.

"Last Tuesday two of our settlement-house boys were arrested for stealing. They admitted they were guilty but refused to say why they did it. I was in court with Mr. and Mrs. Gray, the directors of the mission. Mr. Gray asked that he be allowed to uncover additional evidence. The request was granted and three hours later he was back in court! Their mother needed food! She is in the last stages of TB and hadn't had a doctor. The father deserted them over a year ago and the boys stole rather than go to the authorities, for fear they'd take the mother to the hospital. It's so hard to make them understand why she is there now and why they are there too. Of course both boys are infected, and a large number of us have had to be checked too. I went to see the mother yesterday. She has almost wasted away; but because she didn't understand the language and the people in this new land, she felt safer in her own little room.

"I don't need to write all this to you, Aunt Margaret; you see it daily in your own city and your own clinic.

"There are wonderful things going on in the school. Miss Hester and I are praying about the place I'll go after Christmas. Like the song, I feel I can sing 'My heart's in the highlands, my heart's far away,' because as things stand now, it looks as if the Kentucky hills will be my spot. Yesterday a letter came from Mr. Richards, director of the mission, and he'll take me sight unseen. Come to graduation, please, Aunt Margaret, and let's have a few days together before I go south."

Of course Margaret came, but she brought little news of her brother and his wife. "I did hear that Clark is getting more and more deeply involved in politics and Druscilla is going on a Caribbean cruise. Marcia is back at school in Switzerland but will come home this summer. Sam keeps me informed; he sees them often at the club and pries out any information he may want at the moment. He's the only one I've ever known who can say what he pleases to Clark. I only wish he pleased to say the words of eternal life."

"Someday Daddy will have to listen. Daddy and Mums both. I wish I could take Marcia with me and help her. She's beautiful, Aunt Margaret, and very talented, you know, with brush and pen."

"Someday you may have the chance to reach Marcia." Margaret little realized how prophetic those words were.

12

Land of Hills

"IF YOU SHOULD ARRIVE during or shortly after a heavy snow, be prepared to stay with Mrs. Flora Vinson on Pine Street (right behind the court house) until we can come to you. At times when the weather is bad our mountain paths and roads are impassable for days. This can apply to floodtime as well as snow. This is not written to discourage you, but so there will be no surprise on your part if you should come at a bad time weatherwise." This had been part of a letter Merry had from Mrs. Richards before she left for her new home.

If all went well, she could drive to the very door; if not she would stay in the nearby town, communicate by telephone as soon as possible, and probably make a grand entrance escorted by some of the staff. *I almost hope it does snow,* she thought, *just so I can get acquainted gradually with the town and then go on to the mission. Surely it might help to know a bit more about the foothills before I go deeper yet. I can scarcely wait.*

However, the snow didn't fall until three days after her arrival. Merry drove to the very door of the administration building and wondered at the well-kept brick and log buildings and the happy children as they came scurrying from all directions. Some piled in an ancient bus, while others hurried down shady paths.

Then there were Mr. and Mrs. Richards to greet her. "We've been looking for you since around ten this morning. It's well you arrived before dark. The children were dismissed a bit early, so you'll have to meet the day school in the morning at chapel. You'll see the others at suppertime. Did you have a good trip?" Merry was to learn that Mrs. Richards spoke almost as fast as she thought.

"It was a lovely trip. I bring greetings from the school, bushels of apples from Virginia, and a very happy new worker."

They were laughing as they went up the steps. "I'll show you to your room in a minute, my dear. We are doing the unusual and having a little tea as soon as all the students leave. No one will be kept in today. We want to look at you and talk with you, and you must be exhausted."

"No, not really. I would have been here sooner but I stopped at Keenland."

"The race track in Lexington?" Mr. Richards asked and at Merry's nod threw back his head and roared. "See, sweetheart." He looked at his wife in mock horror. "I told you anyone Hester would send us would be different! Different! Yes, different and interesting." He shook his head and turned into his office.

"Oh, don't fire her yet, Charles. I think horses are beautiful."

Merry grinned at her new friends. "I didn't exactly go to see the horses today. Five years ago when autumn was at its loveliest, I was there at the races with my family. Daddy won an astonishing amount of money on one of the prettiest fillies I've ever seen run. Well, on our way out, he stopped a man whom he thought was the groom. Daddy asked him how much he had made that day and the man said, 'Nothin', boss. I'm just the caretaker. Sometimes I bet but not much,' Daddy gave him a generous tip and the old man kept thanking him. I've always remembered him. He said he wasn't usually around for people to tip him. I've thought of him a number of times lately when I was planning my trip, and when I was so close today I had to go by and talk with him."

"Did he believe?" Mrs. Richards asked, easily skipping the unimportant details.

"Yes. All along he had seen the emptiness of the lives milling around the track. And when I showed him the verse 'I had rather be a doorkeeper in the house of my God,' he said, 'I've got to find out more about doorkeepin'.' Then he took me to his tiny house so I could meet his wife and their little granddaughter." Merry sighed. "This has been a glorious day."

Over tea Catherine Moore told her, "You'll be worked to death." Then she grinned impishly at Mr. Richards. "For six months now he's been saying 'We can't wait for reinforcements. Poor thing when she comes.' "

"In all our correspondence," Merry said slowly, "no one has told me exactly what I'm to do except to have classes three days a week."

"Don't ask," Mrs. Richards warned. "We learned better years ago. It's a sign only that you need twice as much to occupy your time. Merry, if you ever run out of a job, come to me, never to the boss man."

They had to love him a lot to tease Mr. Richards so much; but there was little doubt about it—there was work to be done and this little teatime was a rare one for afternoons at the mission.

"We usually don't get a chance to stop until the dinner hour," Catherine told her.

At dinner that night Mr. Richards outlined more plans for the new recruit. "We'll introduce you to the students at Friday chapel tomorrow and let you talk a few minutes to them. Over the weekend you'll see how the school runs, and Monday you will be ready to pitch into your classes and visiting.

You really came at a good time because we are changing some of our Sunday school classes and you may have your choice between intermediate and senior girls."

Mr. Richards picked up the cake knife and began to serve the coconut-topped cake as his wife handed him plates with home-canned peaches and the mission's own cream.

"You see what I mean, my dear," Mrs. Richards spoke as if in an aside. "He's giving you two days to get settled, a schedule heavy enough to bow a veteran; and he punctuates it with peaches and cake so you'll think you have nothing to do."

"Sensible girl, sensible amount of work." The man was unruffled.

From that moment Merry was not just a new worker but a vital part of the mission family.

She wrote to Margaret, "It's a good thing to come here straight from school because a dormitory of giggling little girls isn't too far removed from the excited students back at school rushing hither and thither. Just in a hurry about different things."

One of the girls whom Merry loved at first sight—and the most—was Lucy, sweet, soft-spoken, with great brown eyes and luxurious curls falling around her shoulders. She was always clean and neatly dressed by any standard. Her clothes were well mended and her hair gleamed. She was never in a hurry to leave when the closing bell rang, but often sat a good hour at her own desk while Merry checked papers or made lesson plans. After a few days of casual and infrequent conversation, Merry realized the girl had stayed, as she had hoped all along, just to talk. True, she had spent her time well, but the real purpose and need were greater.

"Miss Merry," she asked one day, "you reckon it'd be very hard for me to get to be a teacher like you?"

"Not too hard, Lucy. All it amounts to is to do each day's

work well; and if teaching is what the Lord would have you to do, He'll help you."

"It looks hard to me. Some of them words you put up for us are sure hard to remember, and some of the stories you read don't sound real. You sure that one about the Bird fellow really happened?"

"Bird fellow? You mean Lindbergh?"

"Nope. He wasn't that kind of man. I know about Mr. Lindbergh. He flew acrost the ocean. I mean that Bird man."

"Oh, you mean Admiral Byrd? Yes, Lucy. All I read about him actually happened."

"He sure must have studied a heap."

"I expect he studied all his life."

"Don't look like some people ever stop. Mr. Richards, he always carries a book besides the little Bible in his pocket."

"Yes, some people really enjoy studying. Others don't. That's one good reason why there are so many people to fill all the different kinds of jobs in the world. It would be a strange thing if everyone liked to can fruit and no one wanted to plant trees."

Lucy laughed at the very idea. "I never thought of it like that. I never thought much that plantin' was anything special. Now, goin' to new places, that's more like it." She closed her book and began to pull on boots and mittens. "I best hurry. It's a long walk up the path and I got my chores to do."

On a sudden impulse Merry put away her papers and said, "I'll walk along with you. There hasn't been time this week to get far from the buildings. If I don't walk a bit, I'll forget what feet are for."

"Ain't it pretty, Miss Merry?" the girl asked as they began their climb. "Look at all that ice froze on the trees and the snow so hard and white."

"It's so beautiful I'd like to sit down and enjoy it if it weren't so cold, Lucy. My little sixteen-year-old sister paints, and what she does love most to put on canvas are pictures of snow and the sea."

"I wonder what the sea is like. Oh, I've seen pictures in books, but I'd like to hear it. Some say it roars and makes a frightful noise."

"It is very wonderful, Lucy, especially when a storm is coming and the waves are high and angry. Do you have far to go?"

"Not much farther. You'll come in and meet my ma, won't you?"

Merry glanced at her watch. "Yes, I can just do that and get back in time."

"My ma's still pretty, and she don't look old like some women around thirty. She got married when she was goin' on fourteen and she's jus' fifteen years older than me."

Lucy's mother *was* pretty and Merry loved her at once. "Stay to supper. We're goin' to have beans and corn pone."

"I wish I could but I didn't even tell anyone I was coming with Lucy; if I don't get back in time for supper, they'll be out looking for me."

"You stay and I'll have the boys go tell them."

"Let me come another time when I can tell Mrs. Richards beforehand. This is my night to help with the dishes anyway, and I'd not feel right if I left my job for someone else to do."

"I didn't know you teachers washed dishes and worked in the kitchen. Some of the women said as how you did, but I didn't believe them."

"You can well believe it." Merry laughed. "They don't ask me to do anything but dishes yet because the summer I intended to learn to cook, I changed my mind and went to school. Now I think I'll learn right along with the girls in the school."

"Shucks, there ain't nothin' to it. I been cooking since I was ten years old. And Lucy can bake as good bread as my ma herself. What I'd like, Miss Merry, would be to have book learnin' like my younguns is gettin'. Them books mine bring home are the purtiest things I ever laid eyes on. I like most of all their geographies. You know, we never seen a man from China or Japan around here. Some of our men that went off to war said they really do look like the books show them. Said they are right smart. I'd like to know about people like that." She stopped, suddenly embarrassed at having said so much.

"I don't blame you," Merry's tone was casual. "I think I have a book we aren't using right now that you might like to read. I'll send it tomorrow by Lucy. How many other children do you have?"

"Lucy, she's the oldest. Then there's Sam'l; he'll be thirteen come August, and little Janey is ten. We lost two betwixt them two. The twins is eight and they'll be in soon. Then there's Lanney—he's nigh on to seven—and little Cynthie's six. Then we had another set of twins that was both took with a cold and died. This baby is the worst one yet. He's into everything in the cabin. If Cynthie didn't stay by him all the time, he'da burnt himself up or tore up everything I got."

Merry sat in a low homemade chair near the hearth and told them a little story. They edged closer and closer until, at the end, the little children were almost in her lap; and the twins, who came in during the telling, were leaning against the back of her chair.

"I only went for a walk up a little mountain path to share the company of a young teenager, Aunt Margaret," Merry wrote that night. "It was the opening wedge for the work Mr. Richards has had on his heart for years, the beginning of classes for women. Of course they are eager to learn some of the things their children talk about in school, yet with their large and often sickly families, they can't come down to the mission often. We'll begin with those who can, and have girls who are in study hall look after the babies and toddlers the mothers bring along. Once a week we can probably manage it, and it won't be a formal teaching either. We'll sit in little groups, some with sewing in their hands, and we'll talk with open Bibles and, I pray, open hearts. With the new film projector you gave, we'll be able to use many educational aids the state will let us borrow. I'm so excited about this I can scarcely wait for the day to come when we see the rooms full of women eager and anxious to draw others to new fields of learning and progress. These people are so dear, so proud and just plain lovable. Of course we'd probably plan to have classes eventually in different neighborhoods, but you know how scattered they live."

A few days later when Merry went again, Lucy's mother said, "This sure is the prettiest book I ever seen. You sure you don't need it for the younguns right away?" Of course Merry didn't need it, and she told her about the class she hoped to start.

Her eager reply made the girl blink fast to keep back the tears. "I'll come less I got a sick youngun. I'll bring 'em down on a sled as long as the snow lasts. You goin' to talk about it at the meetin' Sunday?"

"Yes," Merry told her, ready to hug the woman for her enthusiasm. "I'm going to make as many calls as I can to the other homes to tell the women about it personally."

"Wonder why no one never thought of this afore now?"

"It's not that they didn't think of it, Mrs. Lee. There just hasn't been anyone to do it."

"Mrs. Richards now, why couldn't she a done it? She coulda talked to us like you say you are goin' to. Don't she know how? And Miss Catherine, she 'pears to me to be right smart."

"Oh, she is and they could. It isn't because they weren't capable, but everyone at the mission has a job and most everyone has taken on an extra one or two," Merry said with a laugh, "or even three. It's something like your job of being a mother, Mrs. Lee. All the time you have is filled up with doing something, and if you had an extra hour you'd find more and more things to do just to catch up. That's why they needed another helper. The Lord chose me and I'm so glad."

"You think He did?"

"Oh, I'm sure of it. My friends and I prayed, and you all were praying for someone. When the dean of women at my school talked with me and showed me the lists she had of places, it seemed God just said, 'Take this one. It's yours.' It's wonderful to see God unfold His plan."

"I'd certain like to know how you think all that. I never seen it exactly in print although sometimes the preacher makes it sound that way. Reckon in this meeting we are goin' to have you could show us how you figure these things out?"

"That would be one of the first things we would want to talk about."

Merry's heart was rejoicing as she went down the hillside.

It was much the same at the other places she visited, except for Mrs. Lacey. "I'd sure like it. It *do* sound so nice, Miss Merry, but this rheumatiz got me so stove up, I don't even get to meetin' except on a Sunday in the summer and then only when my boys fetch me down. I know it's a heap of trouble for them but they do it. Christmas now, they all came here and we went down together."

"Would you like for me to come here just to read and talk with you some afternoon, Mrs. Lacey, and we could have a little meeting all our own?"

"That would be awful thoughtful of you but too much trouble. Imagine all of that for just an old woman like me. No, Miss Merry. I'll wait until spring brings a thaw and then I'll see if I can hobble down."

Merry looked quietly down at the Bible in her lap. "I'd really like to come, Mrs. Lacey."

"Honey, it ain't that I don't *want* you. I jus' think you got others who need you, too; and I ain't aimin' to be braggin', but maybe they need you more. I set a great store by readin' my Bible and prayin'. It's jus' the greatest comfort."

Before she left, their own special prayer meeting time was set, for Merry sensed this would be the powerhouse of her week. They studied together and prayed together, and when Mrs. Lacey found out about a prayer list, she had to write one out. Merry bought a special notebook and a red-and-blue marking pencil.

"Jus' think how easy this will make it. I been tryin' to keep all these things in my head all these years. I aim to fill this little book up right away. First, I'm goin' to set down some of the things I been prayin' for and the Lord already answered. I know He'll keep right on answerin'."

He did. Even Merry, strong in her own faith, marveled at the assurance this simple mountain granny had in God's strength. However, they didn't have their little meetings alone for long. Soon Mrs. Lacey had her sister Emmy staying with her for a few weeks. Then came an elderly cousin from the Bluegrass, a cousin whose son was forever trying to persuade his mother to stay down there with him.

"There jus' ain't no use to it," she complained. "I can't accustom myself to all them people so cluttered up together and nary a thing to do but go down to them big stores and wish you had more money than you got. I don't seem to get close to the Lord in some of them churches, so grand and fine. There were a little one we went to and the preacher spoke so simple-like, but I jus' have to come back home to feel I got religion."

"I'm glad you did. You are like Mrs. Lacey and we need your prayers," Merry told her.

"I suppose you do, honey, but never mind. I'll have to go back some next winter. That boy o' mine sets a store on having me there Thanksgivin' and Christmas, but I'll keep prayin' jus' the same."

There were other cousins whom Mrs. Lacey invited to spend that particular day until Merry explained to Mrs. Richards, "They don't really need me, you know. In fact, another Mrs. Lacey or two and we'd be able to expand our work."

"I wish we could find the other Mrs. Laceys if that were so." Mr. Richards had overheard as he came through the hall. "We had a call only this morning to start meetings twenty-five miles up the creek. We can't refuse it; yet we haven't workers; if we go, it will mean the beginning of a branch school or transporting the children here."

"You're going a long way on one invitation to hold meetings," his wife said.

"I know, my sweet, but you believe it will work out that way too, don't you?"

"Of course. Won't our old bus do, or will we need a larger one?"

"From what the men said, we'll have to get a larger bus after a few weeks. Soon we can go over for midweek services and start real work with the young people. We can take some of our own trained girls and boys over there this summer and have a vacation Bible school if we can fit it in sometime when we won't interfere with the crops."

Merry had been with them two months, so it did not seem at all strange to hear these remarkable people make plans without any time to fulfill them and be fully confident God would make the time as well as provide a man or a staff when the need arose to "go over into Macedonia" to help.

Throughout the day as she went about her own work, Merry began to plan how she could consolidate her own schedule so she too could find some time to devote to this new call. "It's contagious," she told Catherine Moore as they walked toward their cottages that night.

"It certainly is. My brother spent last Christmas here, and now he plans to move his family down in the village in September so he can be on hand to help in the infirmary if we need him. The dear old doctor who has been there for thirty-five years can't go far fast, and not at all after dark. We're liable to have a real hospital here one of these days."

"You mean there's only one doctor on call and he's ten miles away?"

"That's bad? Oh, Merry, think of the people farther up the creek and deep in the hills. Often Mrs. Richards and I were the only ones to answer the calls. We felt really dependent on the Lord, and that is good, but we were two lone nurses where we could have used a hospital. This Christmas when my brother said he'd give up a comfortable practice to work here, we just wept for joy. This is real progress."

13

Man with a Gun

MERRY LOOKED FORWARD to her visits to the homes. Often she had a child tagging along as guide; however, one April Tuesday she found herself unexpectedly free to get into her car and drive as far as possible. She got out and began the steep climb toward a cabin she had not previously visited. The well-worn map supplied by the Richards would be ample guide. It was good to be walking alone along the woodsy path where tiny flowers were just beginning to burst forth and trees were rich in the first unfurling of green. Lines from Pippa came to her lips and Merry half sang, half whispered, " 'The year's at the Spring—the Spring's at the dawn—the Hillside's dew-pearled—and all's right with the world.' Maybe not," she amended, "but please, God, help us do what we can to make it so in this little corner."

She consulted her map, took a turn to the left, walked about half a mile and at a fork in the path went toward the right, following at this stage not the map, but a faint curling of smoke ahead. For weeks she had promised Mrs. Lacey she'd visit her particular friend, an old saint of ninety-seven.

"You'll take to her right away," Mrs. Lacey had said. "She sees right good for her age, but she gets around mighty poorly. 'Pears like she can't put much weight on them thin old limbs of hers. I wish they was somethin' we could do."

"Perhaps there is," Merry mused and talked it over later with Catherine. "Couldn't we get a walker for her?"

"For Mrs. Jones? It's what she needs, Merry, but half a dozen others are in the same fix. At least she has her younger sister to 'do' for her. Some don't."

The answer didn't satisfy Merry. And as she climbed, with her eyes on the soft white clouds, she wondered how she could smuggle in half a dozen walkers without anyone suspecting that her great-uncle's legacy was working again.

"Stand where ye are, or I'll put a bullet through your pretty head." The voice was old, cracked and furious.

Merry whirled around to see a gnarled old man, rifle in hand, eyeing her from one side of a mighty pine. "Yup," he snarled, "I been watchin' you come along, alookin' at that paper. Now you tell me one reason why I oughtn't to bury you here by the path, and I might listen to reason."

"Tell me one reason why you should," Merry replied parrying for time.

"I ain't never seen a lady revenuer but my nephew done talked about how they's women policemen in the cities trainin' to seek out them the men can't find. Why'd they send a pretty thing like you?"

"I'm not a policewoman. I'm visiting or trying to get to see Mrs. Lacey's friend, Mrs. Crawford. Look, I even have some jelly in my bag that Mrs. Lacey sent along."

Merry reached to open her big tote bag, but was stopped by terse words. "Get your hand away from that there bag. You draw out a gun and I'll shoot you afore you could aim it. Looks like you coulda been more watchful. I been trailin' you a good half mile. Seen you when you got out of that fine car. Then I was astandin' by this tree while you stopped and said some fool words and looked at that paper. This here dog of mine made enough noise to make a person look twice, but not you. You jus' kept alookin' at that paper." His hands shook with anger and the gun wavered uncertainly.

"Listen," Merry began patiently, "I'm from the mission. I've only come to pay a visit. I teach the children and talk with the women. Don't you have any of your family in the mission Sunday school or day school?"

"So you want to find out my name, do you? Put that paper down on the stump, then back off so's I can pick it up and read it a bit. I'll take you on up the path a piece and then maybe let you loose iffen you'll promise to keep away from this here place from now on."

"What are you afraid of?" Merry asked softly, her winning smile very sincere as she looked into the old, angry eyes. "Are you afraid I'll visit some of your family? You know, the Lord sent me here and your gun isn't going to stop me." Merry smiled again and the old fellow stood there, belligerent and uncomfortable, as she moved forward to put down the map. "What do you think I have on that map?" At no answer, she continued. "I'll tell you. It's the location of all the homes around here. Yours surely is on that paper too. I know what you are afraid of." Merry had guessed all along, but at last he looked less formidable. "You know, mister, I'm not interested in your still, if that's what's on your mind. I'd not want what's in it if you gave it to me. I didn't even come here to take an ax to it. All I want is to talk to you and anyone else who will listen, but I only want to talk about Jesus."

"You'd likely say somethin' like that."

Suddenly Merry was tired. The day had been long; this was unplanned; she had wasted some time studying the map when she left her car; she had had a very meager lunch and now she was just plain impatient.

With a quick movement, she laid her bag at his feet. "Take it," she ordered. "Now you look inside and if you find a gun or a badge, you are right. If you find a Bible and some jelly, you'll let me go on my way and walk with me so I can read some to you. I'm tired and I'm in a hurry now, and I've every reason to believe when I reach Mrs. Crawford's home, her sister will give me a cup of strong coffee."

The old fellow had kept his rifle leveled at her. But at Merry's rather surprising outburst, he shouldered his gun, picked up the bag and handed it back to her.

"Why a fool woman would carry anything that big lessen she's goin' on a trip's more'n I can see. You're the new one. You're Miss Merry. My Zachey told me about you. Said you're pretty and sweet and patient but once you get riled, you get what you call righteous indignation. Reckon if I walk along peaceful-like, you'll not tell him on me."

"I just might not." Merry laughed aloud now. She had heard of Zachey's granddad. Old Billy was a character who kept more to himself than most. "I wonder why I haven't seen you at the mission. Most of the men come sometime or other."

"Don't seem right for me to come, knowin' all the time I'm aimin' at makin' my livin' at the still. I can talk plain to you, Miss Merry. I heard that much about you. Nope, I can't do no better in ary other way, and I need the money. It's a right good livin' only I don't cotton to drawin' on pretty girls that I mistake for policewomen. Jus' don't tell Zachey, will you, Miss Merry?"

"I'll bargain with you. You start coming to services and you won't have to worry about my telling."

"You mean you'd tell him if I don't?" Uncle Billy handled the old gun again as if for the moment he wondered whether or not he ought to use it.

"I didn't say that."

"I'll come *once*. Here you are. You sure you got some jelly in that there bag?"

Merry opened the bag and took out a little glass of bright red strawberry jelly. "Are you satisfied?"

"I'll be more satisfied tonight when I've got some o' that on my corn pone. You stay and see how good it goes."

"Now I know you are the Uncle Billy I've heard about and that Mrs. Crawford is your sister."

"Heard about me, huh?" he chuckled, then turned serious eyes on her. "I sure am, and if them two women ever find out I drawed a bead on the new teacher, I'll head for the federal jail myself."

"Here, Uncle Billy. Take this little book and read it before you start back to your 'work'."

"Ain't never took to readin'. Can't seem to figger it out."

"You know what you are doing is wrong?"

"Yup."

"And if you get caught, you'll be punished."

"Yup. Iffen I don't get away."

"There's Someone from whom you can't get away."

"Hey? One of them new fellers? I ain't never been caught yet, but three of my partners has been sent away, off and on."

"There is Someone who has already seen you and your still and knows all about you and your partners. In fact, He has His eyes on you right this very minute."

The old man whirled around with such speed, he almost lost his balance. "Where's he at?"

"He's God, Uncle Billy. Don't you know He knows all about you and your business?"

"Never stopped to think on Him thataway. Ain't He got enough to do to take care of them wars and all?"

"It's people who makes the wars; wrong is wrong on a big scale or a small one. Listen, Uncle Billy, I want to read something to you. I want to read to you about the hills and the God of the hills. You know He loves you."

"Nope, you ain't. Reckon I ought to let you go on and find the still and drown in it. I ain't aimin' to hear no Bible readin' and preachin' from a woman. Don't you know I get enough of that mornin' and evenin' in that house?" He pointed out a cabin partly hidden among the trees. "Go on, young woman, and don't tell them nosey females you run into me." He turned to go back down the trail, but stopped for one more word. "Iffen you see me anytime whilst you're there avisitin' jus' don't pay me no mind. Careful with that jelly now."

Inwardly shaking with laughter, Merry hurried on toward the cabin. The old rascal wouldn't hurt anyone.

The fact that he did appear at the meeting the next Sunday added amusement as well as joy to Merry's heart. When Zachary led her to his grandfather, Merry acknowledged the introduction with great cordiality and knew the sigh that escaped from Old Billy was from relief that she had made no mention of their encounter on the trail.

The weeks sped by so rapidly Merry scarcely had time to write the weekly letters she had promised Margaret; often her own mail lay unopened until she went to her room at night. It was the way she wanted it, this being ever so busy and involved in the lives of others that she had no time to think of herself. However, Merry had many, many moments when memory made a great onslaught against her battlements, and always she fled to a quiet place for prayer.

*   *   *

Lucy, who had made rapid progress, began to sit quietly, unresponsive, in class. When school was over, she no longer lingered for long talks but slipped out with scarcely a word of good-bye.

Soon there came days when she was absent and returned red-eyed and even more quiet.

"Were you sick?" Merry asked one day at recess.

"No'm." Lucy looked down at her hands a long moment while Merry waited for the right word to help this child. "Ma don't want me to get married."

"Married! Lucy, you're just fifteen!"

"Yes'm. Ma wasn't that old when she married my pa. She was only goin' on fourteen."

"I thought you wanted to study, to go on to college and be a teacher."

"I thought so too, Miss Merry."

"Then what has changed your mind, Lucy? Don't you still want to learn so you can come back and be a great help to your people?"

"Well, I reckon I do. I like younguns a lot but—"

"But what, Lucy? Is it something I can help you work out?"

"I don' suppose so, Miss Merry. You met Bailey Shepherd in church. He's a widower and he's got three of the sweetest younguns that needs looking after. He's been after me to marry him these last two months. I didn't think much about it until lately. Now I think I'm gonna marry him."

"But, Lucy, he's twice your age."

"He don't look it, Miss Merry. You ever notice his eyes when he smiles? He's real young lookin'."

He was and Merry *had* noticed his eyes when he smiled. And she had noticed more than that; she had seen that his eyes were only for Lucy. What could she say to this child who thought herself a woman? How could she explain all the years of drudgery ahead of her if Lucy herself refused to see it?

"You know, Lucy, your mother has a hard time. She has to work long hours and it isn't easy for her to take care of so many children without help. She has to cook and scrub and wash—"

"Yup. That's the way it is with womenfolk. They ain't got much chance of doin' nothing else, Miss Merry. It ain't easy, but then my pa's always been good to her and she don't complain."

"Don't you think it would be better if you waited until you got more education so you could help your own children more? Lucy, if you learn how to do things an easier way, you can even help your neighbors more. Think of it, if you go on with your studies, you'll learn easier and better ways to can and sew, and better ways to take care of babies so they'll be more healthy."

"I reckon you're right, Miss Merry. You are about some of it." She seemed to be thinking deeply. "But there's one thing you gotta know. I already know how to cook all Bailey can buy. And I reckon if I keep on goin' to school, he'd stop thinkin' about me altogether. He'd start out with some other girl and, first thing you know, they'd be married."

"Have you talked to God about it, Lucy?"

"Well, not really, Miss Merry. Seems like all I can think of is havin' a home of my own and makin' it pretty. And I like Bailey a lot."

They prayed about it, and for the next two weeks Lucy's work improved and she stayed many afternoons to talk with Merry. Each time they got little further than "I guess I ought to wait, but I like Bailey a lot."

Merry went up the hill to talk with the girl's mother. "It's plumb natural she'd think about marryin' now, Miss Merry. He's a good man and a needin' someone to take care of his younguns. Lucy's right handy around the house; I brung her up good. She won't have no trouble atall startin' housekeepin'; besides, Bailey's got more than most she'd marry up with. He's done got his house fixed up right nice and he don't drink."

"It happens all the time," Mrs. Richards consoled her new worker. "They've been marrying young so long, it seems the natural thing to do. Our job is to help them as much as we can and train them after their babies come if we didn't get a chance before. We rarely see them until the children are sick, although of late, Catherine and I have even been called at the time of confinement."

In early May, after a particularly hard week of work and one good soaking in sudden rain, Merry began to cough. In a few days her chest hurt her so much she stopped in the office before school. "I think I have a fever," she told Mr. Richards. "The cough hasn't been bad and last night I thought I was better. This morning my throat hurts and even hot coffee doesn't ease it."

Within minutes Merry was in bed in the infirmary with the old doctor from the village standing over her with a large hypodermic.

"I'm a teacher, Dr. Carlson, not a horse. Didn't you get the wrong needle?"

"You be still, young woman," he ordered, "and sleep as fast and as long as you can."

"Am I very ill?"

"Not in this day and age. I've the cure in this hypo, but a few years ago we would have had a bad time of it with a case like yours. You'll be much better in a few days."

She was, but remained surprisingly weak.

"You'll do no more visitation this term," Mr. Richards told her. "And when the school year ends, you must take a real vacation."

"Oh, no," the girl protested. "I like being propped up against the pillows and doing nothing but read, but I'm really looking forward to the summer Bible schools and learning to can with the women, and picking wild flowers."

"You'll not be here to can," a rough voice boomed from the doorway, and in marched Dr. Sam. He glanced at Mr. Richards and took possession of Merry's wrist. "Fool thing for a delicate child to come here in the wilds and try to kill herself. I'm going to take you home."

"You old darling!" Merry hugged him, thus upsetting his storm. "Mr. Richards, this is my own Dr. Sam and he's a love even when he sounds terrible. He's kind and wonderful and the best doctor in the world."

"Our Dr. Carlson will be glad to lose a patient or two to a man like you. Welcome, doctor. We hope you can stay with us a few days."

"Of course we'll stay. We've come to take care of this child. What did you give her? Let me see her chart. You'll overlook my lack of formality right now. We drove all night."

"Is Aunt Margaret here, Dr. Sam?"

"Indeed I am, darling." Margaret swept in, trailed by a very concerned Becky. "Mr. Richards, I know it must be most disturbing to have a troop of strangers descend on your household, but when Sam knew I was coming, I couldn't persuade him to stay away. I know Merry is in good professional hands here, but he had to see for himself. Now, if you'll put him to work, he'll cause much less trouble and might even go away quietly before too long."

"How did you know I was sick?" Merry asked much later when Dr. Sam had been led off to look at three other cases of flu and a woman with a new baby. "Who wrote to you?"

"I didn't have your usual letter and was just ready to phone when Mrs. Richards called. We didn't have to come, Merry, but—I wanted to."

"Oh, I'm glad you did. I didn't know I had missed you so much, Aunt Margaret. Getting well has been pleasant in a way, but it's hard to lie here and be quiet now that I feel I should be up and about my regular work if only Dr. Carlson would let me."

After two days Dr. Sam left reluctantly to fly back to his own work. "This has been a good change," he insisted over breakfast before he hurried to catch a plane. "First time I've seen patients without any respect for a doctor since I was an intern. I'm coming back, Richards, and live here if my job gets any worse. You know that woman who came in yesterday with the sick boy? She'd been putting turpentine down his throat as well as on the outside."

"It had worked so far, hadn't it?" Mr. Richards asked without a smile.

"Well, the little fellow didn't die, poor chap. No fault of hers though. It would have blistered the skin off an old leather neck like mine. Why it didn't the child's, I'll never understand."

In the infirmary he said a firm word to Merry. "One thing now! You are not to argue with the director of your mission, my girl. You are to come to Margaret's summer place as soon as school is out, and there you are to stay at least six weeks. Those are orders. Understand?"

Later Merry asked, "Do I have to, Mr. Richards? I'm beginning to feel strong again, and I can rest as much here."

"You wouldn't, Merry. I agree with your Dr. Sam. You've worked hard this year, not only here but in school before you came. You haven't had a real vacation for too long. I agree. You have to obey doctor's orders."

Merry made only one stop between her mountains and Margaret's house by the sea. Perhaps this time it was a bit easier, perhaps not.

She had written to Mike's family soon after she entered Bible college. She simply began the letter with what she was doing with no reference to the months since the memorial service. From then on the letters continued to flow as letters do between members of a close-knit family.

This time Merry held Maria's new baby in her arms and looked at his sweet, soft beauty. She held him close to her and wept. Maria came to take the child, but still Merry sobbed. Mama Bernardo sat silently beside her until the storm had passed. Then she stated softly, "You still remember Mike."

"Oh, yes."

"You are indeed my daughter!"

"I am indeed your daughter!" It was a covenant between them, a covenant nothing could break.

Suddenly they were in each other's arms again as they had been the day after Mike had died. The woman wept for her son and the young love he had left, and the girl wept for the grandchild she could not place in those soft, loving arms.

14

House by the Sea

"MERRY, EVERY SUMMER when we came here as children, Mother had an open house, a soiree or a garden party. This year I'd like to revive the custom." Margaret spoke from a lounge at the end of the long side porch. There had been scarcely an idle moment in the day as Margaret went through the yearly ritual of opening her summer home. Of course, a week before, Becky and her Horace had come with an extra maid to clean and prepare beyond the work the year-round caretaker did. However, the day Margaret came was always as special as if she were cutting the ribbon for a new bridge or launching a ship.

Hers was no simple summer home, this huge three-storied house by the sea. The five little guest cottages were overflowing at all times and the four guest rooms upstairs were usually full, even in winter when the house was supposed to be closed. It was as she wanted it—to carry on the grand tradition of real hospitality she avoided during the winter months. However, her guests were not only those one might expect at this fashionable place. Margaret had as her guests the quiet secretaries as well as the bustling society matrons. There were the clerks from the printing houses and bookstores: there were whole families in the cottages, families who would never have gotten away for an overnight trip without Margaret's generosity.

She had a new project this summer. Half a mile from the main house, a large dormitory was almost completed for "little boys," Margaret explained to her niece. There was one large room for the bunk beds, a sunny bedroom for the housemother and father, a kitchen and a huge dining room that served many purposes.

After looking at the nearly completed buildings, Merry teased, "When this is finished, Aunt Margaret, what next?"

"A place for little girls, of course, child." Her aunt laughed with her. "I didn't purchase an extra twenty acres here to farm vegetables."

"There's no end to it, is there, Aunt Margaret? You want many more little cottages and big cottages too."

"Just a few more little ones right away, my dear, just enough to give us all something to do. We'll have a small orchestra from the city to play during dinner and afterward." Margaret was thinking of her party.

"What will we do, Aunt Margaret?"

"We'll get to know our neighbors and friends, my dear. I had thought of having the same caterers I had when Horace and Becky were on vacation several years ago. But when I mentioned that, they were really offended. They insist they can do it much nicer, and I know they can't be surpassed. So the dinner is all in their hands. Then there is a young soprano I met some time ago. She's been studying in Europe these past few years, and I want to introduce her that night."

"Another protégé, Aunt Margaret?"

"Of course. I'm sure she will soon be internationally known."

"And Dr. Sam will be here with his chess set."

"Is he ever without it? However, that will have to wait this year until it is time for people to leave—even if they don't. I've something different planned, Merry. So many people are always busy going to see a play, off to visit an ex-

hibit, watching a ball game, going to a concert, or off to another meeting; this summer we are going to have one good
old-fashioned sing. I've a splendid quartet who will come.
They will lead us in everything from 'Let Me Call You Sweetheart' to 'Roll, Jordan, Roll.' "

Clark Johnson's reply to his sister's invitation was more
than curt. "A weekend in the family summer home under
your sanctimonious solicitude would be more than I could
endure. Even spending one evening at one of your 'little'
parties is out. As it is, I think you've had entirely too much
to say to one member of my family. You've won this hand,
Margaret. We'll see who wins the final game. By pampering
Merry and selling her a sloppy mess of pottage, you've ad-
dled her stubborn, foolish head. But time will tell, my med-
dling sister, time and boredom with your monotonous reli-
giousness."

Margaret didn't show the letter to Merry. She only told
her, "Your father is still bitter, my dear. He has seen nothing
attractive in my way of life since his early teens. We'll continue to pray for him."

The night of Margaret's party the stately old mansion was
splendid by candlelight when the guests began to arrive—the
women in cool summer dresses, the men in trim white coats.
They came from up and down the beach and from the nearby towns, friends who had known and loved Margaret Johnson since she first came, as a tiny child, to stay in the great
house with her parents or grandparents.

As they had seen Merry with her in church, on the streets
going in and out of the shops, and wandering over the countryside, they treated her as if she, too, had always been a part
of the summer colony.

Merry felt a bit of unease at this, her first large party since
the night long ago when her life had been shattered by a
phone call.

In a way, though, she felt like two people: one, the girl

who stood by her aunt greeting the guests; and the other, a strange someone who stood far off to watch the gay people, stimulated by soft music and laughter.

Suddenly she wanted to feel a real part of this happy, laughing party; she wanted to be interested in their gardens, their vacation trips, their houses in town—but she couldn't. *I'm only at home with my mountain children now*, she told herself, as she drifted along the great living room with Margaret's young singer beside her.

"Isn't it wonderful, Merry? A party like this? All these marvelous, famous people have been simply dear to me. When I think of singing for them, I'm almost frozen with fright."

"There's no need for you to be. Aunt Margaret says you'll soon sing for the queen of England."

Then she heard Dr. Sam's gruff voice behind them. "Ever see two prettier fillies, Roger, my boy? This one"—he put his hand on Cherise's head and ruffled her beautiful coiffure just enough to make her wonder if she could get it back in place before she sang—"this one is an import. Margaret tells me she sings like a nightingale and we'll judge that tonight. This one," he said, with his arm around Merry's slender waist, "well, she's one of my own. I've wanted to kidnap her since she was a day old. Now Margaret shares her with me. Oh," he added as if it were an afterthought, "this handsome lad is Roger Blackstone, a doctor of sorts."

"Sam, why don't you go help Miss Margaret with her guests?" The young man moved the tormentor to one side. "I'll see that these young ladies are looked after."

"I must help Aunt Margaret too," Merry said.

"Nope. Dr. Sam is all she needs right now. I'm a man of strong will." Dr. Roger led them away to the beautifully arranged buffet tables and then on to the lantern-lit lawn where the young crowd had gathered.

"You haven't been here in the summer before, have you?"

Roger asked Merry when they were seated at one of the little round tables on the terrace. "I know because if you had been, I would have seen you."

"Not since I was a child. I shouldn't be here now."

"Busy?"

"I live and teach in a mountain school." At the moment Merry wished one of the quartet had not claimed and whisked away Cherise for a dinner partner.

"A missionary?" Merry knew he was appraising her beautiful dress and Aunt Margaret's latest gift, an exquisite dinner ring, an heirloom from her own grandmother.

"Yes. But I had pneumonia this spring and Dr. Sam ordered me to take off part of the summer to be completely idle."

"I'm glad you chose June," he told her, "because I need a skipper for my skiff."

An hour later they moved from their little table, unaware that the quiet-spoken guests knew what they did not—that young Dr. Blackstone was completely absorbed in Merry, the first woman he had noticed since the death of his wife three years before, and that Merry was moving in a dream—quiet and lovely—with stars in her eyes.

When Dr. Sam came to lead Margaret into the music room, she said with tears in her voice, "Sam, they like each other. I know my prayer is being answered."

"Like!" he snorted. "Her feet haven't touched solid ground since she set eyes on the young quack, and he's either hypnotized or slightly feverish."

When Merry heard the first notes of the young soprano's song, she slipped from her perch on the stone wall. "We must go in."

"Wait. We can hear even better out here."

"Perhaps so," she laughed, "but I promised to give Cherise moral support. I'll race you." She did, so that they arrived breathless and just a bit too happy for such a short time together.

The young soprano sang her way into all their hearts. She had chosen her program well for this gala summer night, light songs of love from her native land, enchanting ballads and haunting gypsy airs made all the more enjoyable because she played her own accompaniment on the piano. Last of all she sang Luther's "Cradle Song," and the hush that followed was richer than the earlier applause and cries of bravo.

"She's made now," an elderly dowager said to her handsome husband. "Margaret has a way of finding the most unusual people."

"If she's free, we'll have her out next weekend when the baroness comes," he agreed enthusiastically. "We'll keep her for a real visit too."

All around there were murmurs of pleasure at the magnificent voice and the charming girl to whom it belonged.

Roger and Merry waited for the other guests to offer their congratulations before they went to the piano to speak to Cherise.

As they moved away, Roger asked, "How early may I pick you up tomorrow?"

Merry laughed as her eyes met his briefly then fled across the room. "Early?" she queried. "Am I supposed to know why?"

"Of course. I need a skipper. We'll take a day and sail up and down the bay. What time, Merry? It's just what the doctor ordered." He sounded half serious. "Good salt air, a bit of sea, good food, complete relaxation. What time?"

"Anytime, Roger."

"Nine-thirty be too early?"

"Perfect. I'm so accustomed to early hours I can scarcely sleep past daylight even now."

"Eight o'clock," he amended, "and I'll take you to breakfast at the inn."

Impulsively Merry countered, "Eight o'clock and we'll have breakfast in Becky's kitchen."

Later they moved with the others to the lamplit terrace where the quartet had made a stage of the great porch and begun to sing "Long, Long Ago."

Fascinated, Merry watched as this rather reserved company began to sing with them until soon, from all over, requests were coming as fast as the last notes of a song died away.

"The best evening I've spent since we were here last time," the senior senator said as he took his leave.

"Thank you, Margaret, for bringing us back to simple pleasures." It was a judge from the state supreme court who paused with his wife to bid their hostess good night.

Soon they had all left and the quartet had gone to their cottage. The young soprano floated upstairs on a magic carpet of dreams of more success to come.

Dr. Sam, who was summering at his own place across the bay, said gruffly, "Good night, Merry. I want you to help me with a party sometime. I'd like it to be as capital as this one." He took Margaret's hands and lifted them to his lips. "You were never lovelier, my dear." He was gone before she could reply.

"Don't you love him, too, Aunt Margaret?"

"Love him? Merry, I could never tell you how much. And at moments like this I sometimes even wonder—no, I don't, sweet niece. I know we must wait until he knows Christ as his Saviour too. I've prayed, Merry, oh, how I've prayed; and I do have faith he will be saved. I must have patience, but it is hard."

15

Interrupted Beach Party

MERRY AND ROGER had breakfast in Becky's huge kitchen before anyone else was awake; then they went sailing in the bay. It was a trim craft the young doctor owned, trim and easy to handle for the girl who had spent many of her young summers with boats and horses.

At noon they anchored two miles out and invaded the galley. "I was lazy," Roger admitted. "It was easier to have a lunch put up than to prepare one."

"And *such* a lunch," Merry sighed as they went on deck with heavy trays.

A great calm descended in the afternoon and they were content to let the boat lie quietly in the clear mirror of blue. Throughout the morning as they had raced from one topic to another, Merry realized the glimpse of joy and completeness they had found in each other the night before had limitless horizons. Nor was there any mistaking Roger's every look and gesture. Now for a few moments they were as quiet as the hush before a storm.

Merry, watching while Roger cast his line over the side, sat with her hands relaxed in her lap as he fished with apparent complete concentration. He wasn't thinking of fish alone, the girl knew, for he had a way of glancing at her as if she were some rare treasure he had just discovered. Merry recognized the danger signals in her own heart, and, with a sudden movement that caused Roger to raise a questioning eyebrow, she said, "I must go back now."

"There's no reason to. They won't expect us until sunset." When she only looked at him, the young man asked almost fiercely, "Why?"

She knew she had been foolish to let him see her confusion. Something of the old Merry was in her laugh. "It simply doesn't seem right to be so idle. Even on a summer vacation, I keep feeling I should be accomplishing something."

"You are," he countered. "You are adorning this boat as it has never been adorned before. You are giving me a happy, carefree day with the most enchanting companion I've had in several years; but of course if you want to *do* something, there's a book of verse on the shelf in the cabin. Read to me." It was a command, not a request.

So Merry went quickly to the cabin and there found a volume with a worn cover of old leather. She turned the pages slowly. *How odd!* she thought as she sat beside this strange man and began to read the poems of Christina Rossetti. When she finished "Light of Light" and paused to think about it, Roger laid aside his pole.

"I only discovered Rossetti this past winter," he said. "Of course, I read some of her works in college, but last November an old patient of mine handed this to me with the words 'I want you to have this, and if I'm still here, tell me when you finish.'"

"Was he?" Merry was more interested in the person than the book.

"It was a dear old lady. No. Nor did either of us expect her to be. She couldn't have given me a more perfect parting gift. Do you ever wonder, Merry, at the amazing way God puts together the pieces of our lives to make a beautiful mosaic? Each thing He adds gives us something rich and rare although we don't always recognize it as such at the time."

"And the things He takes away?" The question came quickly, involuntarily, with a passionate fierceness that surprised them both.

"I'm not always sure, though I see it often. A doctor does, you know. But I *am* sure that those who wait upon Him do renew their strength, and I know that the final picture of a Christian's life proves that all things do work together for good to them that love the Lord, to those called according to His purpose." He looked at Merry intently for a few seconds, then asked gently, "Were you thinking of my Connie?"

"No. Oh, no. I'm sorry, Roger. I probably sounded like it. No, I was thinking of something in someone else's life."

"Would you like to talk about it?"

Again she was gay. "No, I'd like to catch one fish before we go in."

Catch one she did and then another and another until Roger teased, "Stop. Either quit catching them or throw them back. I don't want to clean fish all night."

"I'll clean them," Merry promised and meant it. "Where I come from, pardner, we never throws out nothin' fit to eat."

He grinned and began to clean the catch.

*   *   *

Jou-Jou, Roger's young sister, met them at the dock. "We're invited to a barbecue at Dr. Sam's beach tonight at seven; campfire, his specials and all."

"We'll be there, won't we, Merry?" Roger helped her over the side of the boat and jumped to join her. She liked the way he made his decisions and made them for her too.

I'm being foolish, she thought, the words racing back and forth in her mind. But she asked casually, "What are Dr. Sam's specials?"

"Some old sauces he pours all over everything that has an ounce of meat on it. His sauces are hot enough to send anyone to the hospital," Jou-Jou explained, "and we accuse him of using his specials to get patients—but we eat his concoctions just the same. Then he does something to apples and cherries no one else can do. At least he claims the art is his. I've suspected his man may do more than stand by."

"Dr. Sam usually likes us to be there a little early to admire his view," Roger said as he swung along beside them. "I'll pick you up at six-thirty, Merry."

She almost used her stock phrase, "I'm too busy," but she was delayed by the flutter of her own heart. In that instant of hesitation, Merry lost her faint battle of resistance.

"At six-thirty, yes. If I run."

Later in the shower, she told herself seriously and firmly, "This is the last time. Tomorrow I'll begin the work I brought along. I'll finish that correspondence course. I'll start on the little dresses. This is fun, but I know it isn't for me. Yet while I'm a part of it, I shall pretend."

It didn't seem like pretending or dreaming as she walked down the deep-set stone steps to Dr. Sam's beach with the tall, admiring man beside her.

They were finishing the last bit of dessert when Margaret's butler came toward them. "Telegram, Miss Margaret."

However, it was Dr. Sam who reached for the yellow envelope. "Want me to open it, Margaret?"

"If you like, or do I have a choice, Sam?" She was unconcerned as he tore open the telegram. "Well!" Now there was slight impatience in her voice. "Well? What does it say?"

Dr. Sam handed it across the fire to Roger as he answered, "Margaret, Merry, it's Clark. He's been hurt."

"Oh, no!" Merry gasped.

"Let me see!" Margaret demanded as she rose to her feet.

Merry read with her, "'Mr. Clark thrown from his horse while hunting this morning. In Richmond hospital. X-rays show serious fractures. Internal injuries suspected. Please advise. Murphy.'"

"That dear man." Margaret was sobbing. "Sam, can you drive us to the train?"

"Better still, Miss Margaret, let me fly you to Richmond," Roger said from his place beside Merry.

"Please do. We might not be able to leave until tomorrow if we go by train," Merry begged.

Roger led her up the stone steps and along the path. "Pack only what you need. I'll be ready at the airport to take off in forty-five minutes. Can you have them there by then, Dr. Sam?"

"We'll be there, son. I'm going too."

Somehow their bags were packed. Dr. Sam called the Richmond hospital and came away from the phone with troubled eyes. They said little on the way to join Roger in his neat little Cessna.

"Three of us are praying, Merry," Dr. Roger said as he put her in the copilot's seat and prepared for the takeoff.

"And Dr. Sam is wishing," she answered. "What did he find out, Roger? He would only say that Father is desperately injured."

"He doesn't know much more than that. It may have been a freak accident. Your dad is a good horseman, isn't he?"

"Oh, yes. He has rows of trophies."

"I thought so. I know you are tired and you probably think you can't rest; but the night ahead may be rough, and tomorrow will be long and hard. You can sleep."

"I don't think I want to."

"I think you should. You are in God's hands and so is your dad."

"That's what frightens me, Roger. My father has kept away from anything spiritual. He has turned away from God."

"Yet God hasn't turned away from him."

"Suppose he doesn't repent?"

"We can only pray, Merry. Did you ever fly like this before in a small plane and think that someday we won't even need a plane to go faster and farther?"

"You mean when the Lord comes back for His own? For a long time I couldn't really comprehend it, how we can all be caught up in the air to be with Jesus forever. But—" Her laugh was like a bell in the troubled night. "I'm only glad I know it will happen someday. Suppose it were to be right now? Suppose the Lord were to appear in the sky to receive us—"

"Dr. Sam might find it difficult to fly a plane."

"Why is he so stubborn?"

"Pride, I suspect. He's the most lovable man I've ever known, but he's just plain proud of his own intellect. Someday he'll see. He has to."

They were quiet a long time.

"Asleep, Merry?"

"No, but I've rested. And, Roger—"

"Yes?"

"Thank you for bringing us."

"I wouldn't have it any other way. This is where I want to be."

16

Merry's Grief

IT WAS A FAST DRIVE from the Richmond airport to the hospital. Merry noticed the men were unusually silent as they went into the circular driveway, left the taxi and entered the beautiful lobby.

As soon as Dr. Hallack identified himself, there was a quiet scurrying around to contact the doctors he wanted to see. Even in the moment of tension and concern over her father, Merry wondered at the ease with which Dr. Sam could take over a group of nurses and have them act as if *he* were the chief of staff.

In a matter of minutes they were standing outside Clark Johnson's door with the resident physician, who explained, "He's conscious and we are doing all we can to make him comfortable. There's no doubt now about internal injuries, but he's so fighting mad that he's not giving himself much of a chance to recover."

"That's Clark, all right." Dr. Sam spoke meditatively. "You girls stay out of his sight unless he asks for you. In his mood you'd only make him worse."

Just then Murphy came into the hall. "Miss Margaret, he's bad off, he is."

Merry put her arms around the old butler. "I'm glad you've been with him, Murphy. Have you been able to talk to him at all?"

He stroked her hair as he had done when she was a small child and came to him for comfort. "Not a bit of it, Miss Merry. I tried, but he cursed and I just stood there and prayed."

"The fool," Dr. Sam muttered. "He'll kill himself if he has half a chance. I'm going in, Dr. Moffatt."

"Of course, Dr. Hallack." He opened the door and followed Dr. Sam inside.

Sam was gruff as usual when he was deeply moved. "Might be able to talk some sense into his stubborn head," he said.

However, he was completely the sympathetic professional as he leaned over the restless figure on the hospital bed. "Clark, it's me—Sam. Where are you hurt, boy?"

"Hurt? All over! They've shot me full of stuff, Sam, but it doesn't do any good. That horse killed me but not fast enough. I'd be roasting in hell now if she had fallen on me."

"You still have a chance to pull through, Clark. Lie still and let us do what we can for you."

There was a mocking laugh that turned into a groan. "With my bones so cracked up I can't move, and they won't set them until they run more tests and pump more slush in my veins. What are you trying to give me, Sam? None of that stuff. I want Kitten." His eyes were suddenly glazed and his voice sank to a whine and a sob. "Where's Kitten?"

"I've sent for her, Mr. Clark." Murphy, unable to stay away from his employer, stood again at the foot of the bed.

"When's she coming? I want her now."

"She should be here soon. Won't you rest now awhile, sir?"

"Rest? Is there rest in hell, Murphy? You think I'm going there, don't you? And I think I'll fight my way out." He closed his eyes and those around him thought he had lapsed into a coma. Dr. Sam took his wrist gently to check his pulse. "I'm not dead yet, Sam. Just resting. I'm not—going to die.

I'm going—to—do—exactly what—you tell me." With an effort, he forced out the next words. "I'm going to get well and I'll be—governor yet. Murphy, get out—of here. Go put a bullet—through—that horse's head. You—hear me?"

"It's already been done, sir. The horse broke both front legs in the fall."

Again the sick man's voice changed to a soft sob, a whimper, then came a whisper. "Sam—in—my chest. In—my belly. Get—something for me—even if—it kills me. I can't stand this—pain. I've never been—sick, have I, Murphy?"

"No, sir. You've been strong, sir. I'm praying you'll be well again."

"Don't—talk about prayer—to me. What good would—it do to pray to a—God who would—let a man get in this—condition?" Again the words came in a rush. "I didn't have to fall, did I?"

"You fell, Clark. Now lie still." It was Dr. Sam who put a restraining hand on his shoulder. "Here's the nurse and doctor to give you a transfusion. Close your eyes and be still."

"I'll be still soon enough, and you know it. Murphy," he tried to raise himself up, only to fall back groaning on the pillowless bed. "Murphy, where's Kitten?"

"Mrs. Johnson is on her way, sir, with Miss Marcia. They should be here early in the morning. Mr. Clark, will you see Miss Margaret?"

With a string of curses that sent the old man tottering back from his place at the foot of the bed and left Dr. Sam tight-lipped and stern, Clark Johnson tore at the blankets and lapsed into a comatose quiet.

Dr. Sam, the nurse, Dr. Moffatt and the intern worked swiftly with massage, oxygen and hypodermic. Roger stood watching. Merry slipped in to stand beside him. "Why don't you do something?" she demanded with indignation.

He took her arm and led her back to Margaret. "There's nothing more to do, Merry."

"They are working in there. They are trying. Please help them."

Dr. Sam came out just in time to hear those words. "We weren't really trying, Merry, my darling. There was nothing to try for. We were only going through a routine. Clark killed himself when he tried to sit up. Not a one of us had the least hope he would breathe again."

Margaret, dry-eyed and drawn, leaned against the white hospital wall, her hands on Murphy's unsteady arms. The poor old man was sobbing like a child. Finally she heard, "He died cursing, Miss Margaret. He died cursing God."

A nurse put a tablet in his hand. "Dr. Moffatt said you are to take this, Mr. Murphy, and then report to his office."

Roger asked softly, "Will you leave everything to Sam and me, Miss Margaret? Merry?"

"Oh, yes. Please Roger. We must go someplace to wait for Druscilla and Marcia. Perhaps the waiting room down-stairs would be best. They shouldn't come here and not find us." Margaret looked as if she could scarcely stand.

"I'm sorry we have no vacant rooms in the hospital," the nurse said. "It's a wonder we had one for Mr. Johnson. There's been an epidemic of summer flu."

"I'll wait for Mother and Marcia," Merry decided. "Roger, will you take Aunt Margaret and Murphy someplace and get rooms for us all. I'll bring Mother and my sister as soon as they arrive."

There was no need for these plans for, just as Roger was ready to leave with Margaret and Murphy, Druscilla and her younger daughter came.

It was the first time in almost five years that Merry had seen her mother, so she was prepared for some changes. There were none. Druscilla was as petite, as stylish, as beau-tifully coiffured as if she had just left the beauty salon, but Marcia, worry written all over her young face, made a sad figure hurrying behind her.

Walking straight to Dr. Sam who was coming down the hall, Druscilla ignored the others. "Take me to him this minute, Sam. I chartered a plane and we made good time. How is he? Clark never fell from a horse before in his life, did he, Murphy? Didn't you teach him to ride when he was a little boy?"

"Indeed I did, Miss Druscilla." The old man's voice broke.

"Well?" She moved down the hall with an imperious sweep of her hand. "I'm waiting, and I must say you are most uncooperative, Sam. Why don't you say—Sam, he's going to be all right, isn't he?"

"Druscilla, sit down."

"You aren't going to tell me Clark is badly hurt, Sam. Margaret, have you talked with Clark?"

"No, Druscilla. Sit down and let Sam tell you—"

"Tell me! Tell me!" Her voice rose to a hysterical pitch. "I don't want anyone to tell me anything but that he's all right and he's going to ride again and walk and dance and—"

"Mother," Merry stood in front of her and tried to take her ever fluttering hands. "Daddy isn't—"

"Go away, Merry. I'm going to think only good thoughts, and you made Clark unhappy. I want—"

Somehow Dr. Sam was able to usher them into the upstairs waiting room. He stepped into the hall, held a brief conversation with a passing nurse, and was back in seconds. This time his voice was even more firm than usual as he took those silly, useless little hands in his big ones and drew Druscilla to sit beside him on a couch. "Druscilla, Clark was very badly hurt. He had a rough fall on a rock fence, and there was little we could do for him."

"He'll be better just from seeing me. I know he will." She tried to stand, but the old friend held her beside him.

"Roger, I've ordered a sedative," he said as the nurse appeared in the door, hypodermic in hand. "Administer it,

please. Druscilla, you must listen to me. We will all help
you. Clark could not get well."

She looked at him dully and made no move of protest as
Roger inserted the needle, then massaged the spot with the
little piece of cotton.

"Oh," she said slowly after a few seconds, "of course, he
couldn't get well with you two able-bodied doctors not doing
a thing for him. I'll go to his room. When he has headaches,
he always feels better when I massage his head. I understand
Clark. Coming, Marcia?"

The young girl was weeping in Margaret's arms. "Mother,
don't you understand? We didn't get here in time."

Now there was shrill laughter. "Of course I understand.
They have been trying to say your father is dead. Stupid!
Stupid! I'd never believe such nonsense. Clark can't die.
No—" Her voice became thick and slow. "No—Clark is go-
ing—to be governor—I'm to wear a—rose gown—a—rose—
gown and dance in the mansion."

"Will she be all right?" This from Margaret as she bent
over her sister-in-law.

"I'm not sure." Dr. Sam was checking her pulse. "She
would not accept anything we had to say. She is trying to
escape into a far corner of her mind, into the dream she
would like to make reality. She knew Clark was dead but
she would not let us say the words."

In a few minutes Druscilla was installed in the same quiet
room in which her husband had died. She lay there, sleeping peacefully with round-the-clock nurses at her side.

"We'll be back," Dr. Sam told the resident physician, "as
soon as we can make arrangements and get some rest." He
ushered his sad little group out of the waiting room and down
the corridor.

"Why wouldn't my mother listen?" Marcia asked when
they were in the cab on their way to the John Marshall Hotel.

"I'm not sure. Druscilla has never had a problem she had

to face alone in all of her life. Her parents first and then Clark took care of her." He looked thoughtfully at Marcia. "How did she accept Murphy's phone call, angel?"

"She was playing bridge with the Maceys when she was called to the phone. I was at the pool just ready to dive in when Mr. Macey came to get me. When I went in the room, I heard Mums saying, 'It's all nonsense, of course. Clark went to Virginia on business. He usually joins a hunt if he has time and gets a chance. He couldn't be badly hurt.'

"Mr. Macey told her, 'I talked with Murphy, Druscilla. He seemed unusually worried. I think you should go at once.'

"Mums looked annoyed. She answered, 'Of course I'll go at once. You'll get a plane for me, won't you, Bill? I know though that Clark isn't seriously hurt. I don't care what Murphy says. Will someone pack for Marcia and me?' "

"And on the trip?" Roger prompted.

"She was terribly nervous although the doctor there had given her something before we got on the plane. She kept saying, 'Clark will be fine when we get there. He won't even have to stay in the hospital. Clark can't abide a hospital anyway. I'm glad we got off in a hurry.' Dr. Sam, my mother isn't going to die, too?"

"No, little one, your mother is just terribly upset. Now we are all going to have a good breakfast sent to our rooms, rest a long time and talk of what we have to do later."

What could she do for this young sister whom she hadn't seen for almost five years? Merry wondered as they sped on their way. The first move was not hers. It could not be. Marcia looked at her sister with frightened eyes. "Let me share a room with you, Merry. I don't want to be alone."

"I'll like that, Marcia. We've a great deal to learn about each other, and many things to settle."

However, it was easy learning to know this young girl, because Marcia was terribly tired of the life she had been living. After the year in Switzerland, she had spent her winters in an exclusive school in France and her summers and holidays in the shadow of Clark and Druscilla and their ever exciting search for a new thrill or triumph.

That night, alone in their room, they had talked for hours when Marcia suddenly exclaimed, "Honestly, Merry, I don't know how you managed to persuade them to let you stay with Aunt Margaret, but it must have been heavenly to feel you *belonged* someplace. Merry, why did you ever decide to go and live in the mountains?"

Merry told her of her wish to help others because she loved the Lord Jesus. The girl listened with a new light in her eyes at the wonder that God had called her sister to a special work and had shown her the way.

When she asked, "How could you know about God? How could you be sure?" Merry explained His Word, and Marcia believed.

It was so simple, so lovely, and yet so utterly surprising, Merry could not wait until morning to share this new joy with her aunt.

That night after her sister was asleep, she slipped into Margaret's room. "I think she's been waiting for this a long time, Aunt Margaret. I didn't need to tell her very much, just answer her questions. She said she wants to go back with me when I go home to my hill children. She wants to live at the school and finish her senior year there. Do you think Mums will let her?"

"I think that will be your decision, Merry. Druscilla may never be well again. Sam and Roger told me they have known a number of cases like hers. Recovery is very rare. She has always been an escapist. With Clark's death, her means of escape has disappeared."

So it was. When Druscilla Johnson awoke from her drugged sleep, she told the nurse, "I'll have breakfast in bed this morning. You know I must rest. Mr. Johnson is to be inaugurated as governor today, and there will be a lovely ball. Tell Murphy not to call him. I want the new governor to sleep as late as he can. We'll be dancing until morning. Would you like to see my gown?"

It was much the same when Margaret and Sam went in to see her later in the morning. But when Merry went in, the gay little woman became stern. "I wish you'd stop coming home, Merry. Now of all times your father must not be upset. Go someplace and let us alone. Merry, you are so selfish. It's very wrong of you to be serious and so religious. You'll spoil the inauguration. Did you see my rose gown?"

"No, Mums. I'll go now."

To Merry and Margaret the tragedy of Clark's death was almost more than they could bear. Because they had prayed so long and so earnestly, they had felt he would turn to the Lord. Yet, they remembered that each time they had talked to him, he had been more and more hard.

Clark Johnson was buried with a simplicity he would have scorned. His grave was smothered with costly flowers sent by wealthy and famous friends from across the nation. Many came to pay homage to a man they admired, feared and followed. Certainly many were astonished at the gospel message instead of a eulogy of the dead man; but they could not have gone away untouched by the old, old story the young minister told.

Marcia was almost dazed by the sudden bereavement, for she had lost both parents in one day. On the other hand, she was so thrilled with the love of God for her and so happy with her sister and aunt and the interest they were showing in her as a person, she could not be wholly sad.

"The best thing for Marcia will be to become absorbed in the activities of the high school crowd," Roger had said on their trip back to the beach. "You just watch those kids at work. I called Jou-Jou last night. She'll take care of her."

Soon they had all settled down to the relaxed routine of

summer—only there was not now the same spontaneous gaiety they had had before.

The first night back Merry escaped from the house, sped down the stone steps to the beach, paused, changed her mind, and hurried back to the stone-walled garden. There she sought refuge under a huge oak tree and let the pent-up tears flow, the agony of suppressed grief shake her. She had held herself in check for the sake of Marcia and their aunt. She had felt she could stem the tide of sorrow, but since their return to the seaside, she had been beset by the cry of her heart. Now the words came out. "It seems such a waste, Lord. I thought my—suffering could bring my parents to Thee. If I hadn't feared my father, I would have married Mike and that little boy would be mine still. Oh, dear Lord, why? Why? O God, Your ways are not our ways, and I don't have to understand. I only have to trust and I—do. I'm not rebelling, I just wish I could go back in time to have known Jesus sooner. Thank You for Him. Thank You for His soon coming."

But she continued to weep as if she could never stop. She was unaware of anyone else in the garden until Roger touched her arm. "Merry, cry if you must, but crying like this won't undo the past few days. You can't help your father by grieving."

His words, his presence, were a complete shock. As suddenly as the storm had engulfed her, the tears and sobs stopped.

"I didn't know you were here."

"I just came down from the house. I was looking for you. You've been very, very brave."

"No." She turned to look over the garden wall and gripped the cool stones until her hands ached. Roger thought she was mourning for her father and that alone. She could not tell him that her tears were for him—her mother—and herself.

Merry wept again, great choking sobs she could not stifle. Suddenly she was within the comfort of strong arms.

"Merry," Roger was saying, "I would do anything to make it easier. You simply have to realize you did all you could. Grieving will only hurt you, not help anyone." His tone became even more serious and deep as he added softly, "But if you must weep, Merry, weep here."

His words were no surprise nor was it strange to be in the shelter of his arms. From the moment they had met such a short time before, and in spite of the tragedy of the last few days, Merry had known that this man was not just another friend, but someone special she had not expected to find.

But she would not be special to him; she could not be when he realized she was not bowed with filial grief but mourning for a bit of her own life she could not change. Then there flashed across Merry's mind the firm resolution she had followed since Bible school days. She had work to do; she would do it with the Lord alone. Not even in her thoughts did she form the words of the prayer she sent up to her heavenly Father, but the answer came back as clear as the soft winds from the ocean. "I am with you always." This promise of Jesus was hers to claim anew.

She accepted Roger's handkerchief, dried her eyes and told him quietly. "I'm all right now. Thank you, Roger. I needed to—think."

They talked there of many things before they went up the walk to the house.

"I'll call you tomorrow," Roger said as he left her at the door. "Will you rest now?"

"Of course. Good night."

His call came early, but it was not what either had expected it to be. "I've been summoned back to the city by a very sick patient who doesn't believe doctors should take vacations. Get ready for another day on the boat, Merry. Promise?"

She would miss Roger unbearably, but she was glad, Merry told herself, that he had been called away. It gave her time she needed so desperately to consider many things—her own responsibility to Marcia, her renewed promises to the Lord, and the quiet rest she needed.

However, again and again Merry's sleep was interrupted by the nightmare of her father's death. Then she would awaken to the sound of her own sobbing. It would be an hour or two before she could read herself to sleep.

Dr. Sam scolded her about the circles under her eyes. "I ordered you to come here to recover from a hard illness. I know you've had a shock, child, but you are making yourself sick."

"I don't intend to. It's the dreams. Almost every night I wake up weeping after a terrible dream of Daddy and the things he shouted as he was dying. I think I'd like to go back to the hills sooner than you said I could. Work would be good for me now. I've only to close the house in town."

Dr. Sam wouldn't listen. For one thing, he was thinking of Margaret and the pleasure the girls brought to her by just being there. "You stay on a while, Merry. You are a comfort to your aunt, and she's good for both of you girls. The main person to consider now is Marcia, and I can tell you she needs to be with this young bunch. Call it what you want; if it is Christianity that is helping her, it's good. They speak her language a little better than you and Margaret do. Give her a little more time here."

Merry and her sister did not go back to close the house in town as they had planned. In preparation for the trip, Merry wrote a letter to Murphy. "The doctors give little hope that Mums will recover, at least not without much time and treatment. We want to keep the house just as it is for her, however, in case there is a time she can return. Of course, even if she gets well, it may be too painful for her with all its memories of Father. Marcia is going back with me to my mission field. If you and Mrs. Murphy would like to close the main part and stay on to care for the rest of the house, that will be fine with me. If, on the other hand, you do not want to stay on there alone, let me know. Perhaps you would have someone in mind who would like to take care of it.

"Marcia and I want you to know we love you and Mrs. Murphy and are happy to be absolutely sure that we four are really in the same family—the family of our lovely Lord—after all these years of living in the same houses. With love, Merry."

The letter that came back sent the girls into a transport of joy and planning that was hard to stop. It was a simple one-page note written with great sincerity. "Mrs. Murphy and I have been talking about what is ahead for us. We talked about it even before your letter came and we have a plan that may be good. We've a bit of money put aside for we've had few expenses through the years. We'd like to take some of it and buy a little plot of ground and build a cabin on your mountain where I can have a bit of a garden and perhaps help the lads with some scientific farming. It has been my hobby to study it all these years. Mrs. Murphy would like to help when she can with the baking at the school. Perhaps in her own small kitchen she could bake pies and cakes and maybe take in a few girls to mother who need it more than others; or there might be a need for an old-fashioned parlor where lads and lassies could meet to talk over a cup of chocolate and a cookie. A very fine young veteran is going to our church, and he needs light work. The caretaker's job would be fine for him right now."

17

Walk on the Beach

MERRY TOLD ROGER about the Murphy letter over coffee on the terrace. "I wired back at once. Mrs. Murphy is to pack our things and send them on; Mr. Murphy will hire the young man and see that someone comes in to help him occasionally. Then they will begin the second phase of the mission work. You know, Roger, they've always been at it, only in a different way."

"Won't it be hard for them to be transplanted?"

"Not if they're near Marcia and me. I never realized it fully before their letter came, but until I came to live with Aunt Margaret, they were the only real family I had ever known. We've decided they are to be our adopted grandparents."

They rode on the beach road until the moon was high in the summer sky and talked of everything, even Marcia.

"She's so happy she can scarcely contain herself," Merry said. "She comes to my room and talks half the night. Then she keeps herself busy with the young crowd and has started real Bible study with your sister. Jou-Jou has been wonderful for her."

"Jou-Jou is pretty wonderful anytime. So are you, Merry. Marcia is a fortunate gal."

Merry was floating in the pool the next morning when she heard him call, "Miss Margaret invited me to swim anytime, but that was a year ago so I'll ask you now. May I come in, Merry?"

"If you can stand a lazy swimmer. I'm going to do more lying in a lounge chair this morning than swimming. I'd rather bask in the shade than race."

"Not a sun worshiper, are you? Not if you plan to sit under a maple tree."

"Oh, in winter I seek out old King Sol."

"Be lazy this morning if you like," Roger conceded as he joined her on the float, "but give me this afternoon."

"I couldn't. I'll let you have a spot by the pool, though."

"You mean it, don't you. You want to stay here in Miss Margaret's splendor."

"Aunt Margaret has a bad headache. That's all she'll say except for me to go out and have fun. She looks dreadful and sounds worse. I may not help her any, but I want to stay nearby."

"I'll have a look at her," Roger said, preparing to leave the float.

"Better not try. I doubt that she'd let you. She wouldn't take anything, and she very firmly ordered Becky, Horace and me to let her rest. She said that if she thinks a doctor's visit is advisable, she'll call one; and that applies to you and Dr. Sam."

He laughed. "My hat's off to Miss Margaret. I've known her too long to doubt that she means what she says. I'll join you this morning—you couldn't run me off! But this after-noon I'll have to keep an appointment I made weeks ago. Merry, I want you to go with me and become acquainted with my son. As I mentioned before, he's been with Connie's parents all this past month. I'm going after him today, and we're going to the village fair, ride on the Ferris wheel, see the cattle and pigs and lambs, and eat popcorn and hot dogs. Merry—" He was much too serious for the glaring summer morning. "I want you two to be friends."

"I'd like to meet him, Roger. I especially like little boys."
There was memory in her words, longing in her heart.

"What about big ones?"

"Oh, they'll do," she conceded as they left the float to swim toward the chairs and the iron table where trays of sandwiches, tea and cake were being placed.

"Let me look at Miss Margaret and then whisk you away," the doctor insisted when it was time for him to leave.

"Not today."

"Tomorrow?"

"I've told Jou-Jou the only way I can be seen these next few weeks is by way of sewing machines and scissors."

"How so?"

"There are at least three dozen little dresses to cut out and machine stitch before August ends. Sewing is the one domestic art I took time to learn while I was in Bible college. When I take them home, the women can do the handwork."

"Why three dozen?"

"Someone gave us that much material and patterns. A good beginning for our winter needs."

"Are you serious, Merry?"

"Never more so. You work in clinics on your days off, don't you? There is no difference. I've really convalesced, you know, and I need to keep busy. I'd go back now except that Dr. Sam and Aunt Margaret would throw fits, and Marcia is doing so well here I think she needs a bit more time with these young people before I take her into a completely new world. Besides, Dr. Sam has threatened anything—including a trip to the mission himself—to drag me back when I mention going before the end of summer."

"Bless Dr. Sam. Merry, I can't let you go back, not even at the end of summer."

She looked across the calm pool and slowly brought her eyes back to meet his. "That's a long time ahead, Roger."

"And in the meantime—"

"I'll cut and sew." She interrupted the words he might say. "I'll do the cutting if it has to be done." Roger made a wry face as he pantomimed bending over a table, scissors in hand.

"How could you?"

"I cut more delicate material than cotton and linen almost every day. You be ready with long tables tomorrow morning. No, don't bother. I'll speak to Becky." His fingers touched her hand and Roger was gone with the words "I want you to have free days to play with me this summer."

"He's mad, Aunt Margaret. He'll never come to cut out little dresses," Merry told her aunt later.

"He'll come, and you will be glad."

"I don't want him to come. I think I must go home to my hills right away."

"Don't run, my dear. There's no reason why you can't have a happy life of your own."

"No reason?" Her voice was close to bitterness. "I'll find my happiness in the lives of others. Oh, Aunt Margaret, I don't want this young man to be nice to me—to look at me as if he thinks I'm lovely. I don't dwell on the past, but the decision I made so long ago has to stand. I'll never marry, even if it hurts sometimes to lead a lonely, longing life although my life is full and blessed. Contradictions, Aunt Margaret? Oh, I'm truly not unhappy. I do have the peace that passes understanding, and I love my work. That's where I have to leave the whole matter. I feel it so strongly; that must be the answer."

"If it is lonely and full of longing, my sweet, don't you think the Lord would have you fill the emptiness?"

Merry changed the subject skillfully and quickly. "I'm not living sadly, Aunt Margaret. I rejoice every day at all the lovely things God has given me, all the glorious opportunities to serve Him, and most of all I rejoice that I know

Him. I suppose I've had a touch of vacation blues. I'm going to walk by the sea."

Even as Merry ran down to the shore, storm clouds were beginning to form above the white cumulus drifts. She touched the sand only lightly and rushed along with one promise after another tumbling from her trembling lips. Suddenly she sank down on a little mound of sand and prayed half silently, half aloud, "Dear Lord, I belong to You. You *are* my resting place. Let me be content with whatever You want for me. Keep me ever close to You. In Jesus' name. Amen."

"Why you cryin'?"

There before her stood a little boy, shovel and bucket clutched in his hands.

"I didn't see you." It was an inane thing to say.

"Nobody sees me today. I've runned away. I'm a pirate. Want to come on my ship?"

"Of course I do. Where will we go?"

"To magic land."

"My name is Merry. What is yours, Mr. Pirate?"

"I'm Keith. My daddy's goin' take me see the cows."

Then the call came, plaintive, anxious. "Keith. Come here to Mandy. Keith!"

"Answer her, darling," Merry urged.

"Don't want to. Don't want to go back till my daddy find me."

"Keith, where are you hidin'?"

"Here," Merry called. "He's safe."

The youngster looked at her with reproachful eyes. "You told."

"She's worried. She thought you were lost."

"Wanna be lost." He jumped up and began to scamper away.

Merry grabbed him by his little sunsuit and cuddled him in her hungry arms as his nurse came over the sand dunes.

"I was so scared. Thank you for savin' my child. You're Miss Margaret's little niece, aren't you?"

"Not so little anymore," Merry answered, laughing. "How did he get away?"

"There's no accounting for this boy. I had put him to bed for his nap. Usually he sleeps two hours. Today I started to fix lunch. I turned around and Keith was gone. Mr. Roger loves this little child. I remember the day he brought him home. He picked up Miss Connie early. She was so happy she couldn't sit still the whole morning before he came. Then they drove to town to get this precious baby. I had fixed up his room so much that it was about the most wornout nursery on the beach. Well, come on, Keith. Your daddy is going to be ready to go."

The girl sat looking after them, wondering again in her heart, *Is this my child?* How many times had she asked herself that question about how many little boys she would never know. Suddenly she sprang to her feet to run after the woman and the boy.

"He's very small," Merry gasped, aware of her haste, the tumbling words, the urgency of the questions to come. "How old is he? When's his birthday?"

"He's almost four now. He'll be four on July 20."

The nurse didn't see Merry's hands tremble because she and the child continued toward their home with only a look back to wave and smile.

Finally Merry found herself sitting alone on Margaret's porch without knowing how she had gotten there. There was too much confusion in her mind even for her thoughts to be coherent.

The child could be her little boy. She had to know! But how could she? Wouldn't it be better to remain in doubt than to open the old wound and have no hope of its healing? She could never have the child back. If he were her own, the doctor would never give him up; and the light of love that shone in his eyes for her would turn to contempt. Merry moaned softly. She could not go on like this. If she could only *know*, she might be able to content herself with keeping in touch, seeing him occasionally, having an hour now and then in the summer on the beach. As he grew older she could be his friend. He might think of her as an aunt. Of course he'd be sent to the best schools, but she could write to him, send him cookies and little surprises.

"Why, Merry, you're crying." She hadn't heard the footsteps nor was she aware that her hands were clenching and unclenching in her lap.

"I'm tired, Aunt Margaret. I walked on the beach and I'm tired. I think I'll go to my room until dinner. You're better?"

"Of course. I just get lazy sometimes. Darling child, are you sure it's rest you need? Would talking help?"

"Thank you, Aunt Margaret. Today I'll rest."

At dinner she was her gay self and even pretended to enjoy the excellent dishes Becky had prepared with loving hands.

Their meal was interrupted by a phone call for Merry. "This is Jou-Jou. That brother of mine got in early from the fair and was at the phone to call you when he had an emergency call. Some big wreck on the highway and the operator called even the vacationing medics. He wanted me to beg, plead and entreat you to let us pick you up and take you to the beach for an impromptu bonfire." Her voice was lilting. Jou-Jou didn't bother to hide her interest in her brother's new date. "Marcia already has a date and will join us later. Can you be ready by eight, Merry?"

"Not tonight. Thank you. I have to finish some work."

"Not *at night!* Come on!"

"I'm sorry, but you see I'm a bit behind. And tomorrow I've a full schedule planned so if I don't work tonight—"

"Oh, Merry, Roger will kill me for flubbing the invitation.

I know he thought you'd enjoy being there early or he would have told me to ask you to wait at the house for him."

"Have fun, Jou-Jou. And thank you. I mean it about the work."

"I know you do. But you don't need to bother. Roger has ordered us all to help tomorrow. That idiot brother of mine has even commandeered six sewing machines. Your aunt will *succumb*. I hope you can stand the mess he's going to bring. So with all that, you *can* be free tonight."

"You are sweet to insist, but I simply can't. I'm taking an extension course which I should finish next week."

"But you don't have to, do you?"

"No. But—"

"Oh, Merry, live a little. You're too young to bury yourself completely."

"As if I have. I've played much too much already this summer."

"But you're only twenty-two, and here I'm worried because I'm an old maid of nineteen. Let's play *all* summer."

Merry would not give in. She couldn't just now. She went back to the table and told it all to Margaret.

"Why don't you go out with the young crowd? As Jou-Jou said, you don't have to bury yourself."

"Ah, Aunt Margaret— I'll beat you at chess."

Surprisingly enough, she did, just as Dr. Sam came stomping in the door and claimed her chair.

"She's much too serious for her own good," Margaret said.

"It's not being serious about her work that bothers me. That will make her happy. It's that she won't allow herself to have a life aside from that work."

"Roger may change her mind, Margaret," Dr. Sam said wistfully. "He may be more successful than I."

18

Roger's Scissors

BECKY AWAKENED MERRY at seven the next morning with a tray in her hands.

"Why, Becky, I always come down to breakfast."

"Not this early and not today, child. I can't have folks cluttering up my kitchen. I'm going to take Miss Margaret's toast to her in about an hour. I hope you like your eggs this way," she continued. "Then you hurry down looking mighty pretty."

"Becky, is Dr. Roger here already?"

"To tell you the truth, honey, he said he'd have his crew here by seven-thirty. I thought I'd better get you up."

The eggs were perfect, as Becky's eggs always were, but Merry hurried too much to appreciate them to the fullest.

Downstairs she found the large dining room and the sun parlor being turned into a veritable sewing factory. Someone had carried down her box of materials and patterns, and there stood Jou-Jou with Marcia beside her in the kitchen door.

"That brother of mine!" It was one of Jou-Jou's favorite expressions. "He said it would do us good to see how early girls who sew for a living have to start. Said we'd appreciate our own clothing more. I'm going to nap on that couch." She yawned and headed for the sun porch.

"Oh no you don't." Roger came up, whirled her around, gave her a little spank and sent her toward one of the busier tables. "Well, boss, tell us where to start," he said to Merry. However, in the end, it was the young doctor who set the tasks as well as the pace for the day. By noon Merry's work was finished.

"Now I know why I took home ec," Grace Sherrill sighed as she straightened her weary back and handed the last beautifully stitched blouse to Tim Fredericks and his fiancée, the packers for the project.

"Come on, Merry," Roger said, "everyone is invited to my house for lunch, and you are the guest of honor." At her look of hesitancy, he laughed. "You can't claim a lot of work. You owe us your company, me especially, for the rest of the summer in payment for all the hard labor we've done. Yes, I think I'm especially to be highly rewarded. Don't you know I had to bribe every one of these lazy fellows and gals?"

She looked at them all, these carefree, happy young friends, these lovely rich young Christians, and declared, "I want to make a speech."

They shouted, "Hear! Hear! Speech!"

"Seriously—" She held up her hand. "You've done a wonderful thing and I thank you. There's nothing I'd rather do than have lunch with you all."

Again they shouted and applauded until Becky came from the kitchen to shake her head in delight at the fun they were having and the color in Merry's cheeks.

So they trooped out to the shiny convertibles, the little foreign cars and the two Chrysler station wagons.

"I promised Keith he could eat lunch with us," Roger said as he led Merry up the steps to the beautiful old house she had often admired from Margaret's second floor. "He told me about the lady on the beach. He wants to find you there again. Won't he be surprised when he sees you in a few minutes here in his own home?"

They went through the great hall into the charming living room that looked like a neat Victorian print, but Merry didn't see the rosewood sofas, the satin beauty of the grand piano, or the rare chests and tables brought back from far ports on trading ships long ago. Above one small table, by a wing-backed chair, hung a perfect portrait of a very tiny baby whom she knew at a glance to be the child she had lost.

It was all true then—the age of the child, his birthday, this picture. Of course Aunt Margaret and Dr. Sam had known all along. But what could they expect of her? This had been deliberate, throwing her with Dr. Blackstone, this personable and dedicated Christian. They had meant to be kind, but the pain of it overwhelmed Merry.

Her only desire was to run—run from every human contact—run and not come back to this lovely place and the man who had measured her with his eyes and his heart and found her utterly desirable.

They were alone in the great room, for the others had scattered even as they left their cars. Roger was looking at her with that gaze of admiration again, pleased at her absorption in the portrait of his little boy.

"That was Keith when we first got him," he explained. "We had a good photographer out the next day, and within a week there were eight fine likenesses. So when the portrait painter was ready, he didn't need to interrupt the baby's schedule to accomplish his work easily and well."

Still she did not speak, and Roger touched her arm. "You like it?"

"It's lovely," Merry breathed. "It looks so real." Then she was saved from the flood of tears by the rush of a little boy.

"Daddy, you came and bringed the beach lady, too. I'm going to sit by you," he announced, taking her hand.

"Please do," Merry replied and thought how weak were the words, how emotionless compared to the cry of her heart.

"Now can we eat?" he coaxed. "I'm so hungry. I want ice cream, Daddy. Is there ice cream today?"

"There usually is." Roger swung the child to his shoulder and led Merry to the terrace where tables were set under the trees.

"Tomorrow will you come to my birthday party?" Keith asked suddenly.

"I'd love to come to your birthday party," Merry told him with a mist of tears so blinding she trembled for fear the others would notice. But they didn't.

"I wish you'd help run this party, Merry," Roger asked. "It's the first juvenile one I've ever faced alone."

"Alone? Where will Jou-Jou be?"

"His birthday isn't tomorrow, of course. Mother is coming down and the two of them are planning to join Father in New York to go to Europe for a few weeks before Jou-Jou goes back to college. My talented sister had complete charge last year. I simply looked on."

So it was settled.

Later in her own room Merry knelt by the canopy bed. "Dear Father, I thank Thee," she whispered, "for letting me know where he is and how he is. O dear God, I praise Thee for Thy goodness. Thou hast let me see him." Now the sobs broke forth and torrents of tears streamed down her cheeks. "Please bless him. I thank Thee that I know he has a Christian home and, heavenly Father, I know there are many who do not know where their little children are. Bless and comfort them. In Jesus' name. Amen." When the sobs had subsided, she spoke again to her Lord. "Thank You that I can have him a little while this summer. Somehow the days ahead will be easier. O God, how great Thou art and how kind!"

Margaret noticed a difference in Merry but made no comment even to Dr. Sam. She was almost holding her breath these days as she prayed and watched and prayed again.

It was practically impossible for Merry to escape even a few hours from participating in the summer fun and work of her aunt's small colony. Margaret herself was busy from morning till night arranging outings for the children in the dormitories, picnics and tours for her houseguests, boating parties in the early morning or cool evening. She gave small, informal teas, visited old friends in the village, met trains, buses and planes.

At the end of one busy day, Merry sank beside her at the pool's edge. "However do you manage to survive your summer vacation, Aunt Margaret? If there were two of you, you just might get all this done without making everyone wonder, but only one little lady can't do all the things you accomplish. Aren't you exhausted?"

"Of course not, child. I'm enjoying the best time of my life. This summer has really been rich with you and Marcia here. Don't you know you've done more than half the planning, meeting and picking up? I asked the Lord to let me serve Him these three months in a very special way and, if it is His will, to strengthen me for the winter ahead. I know He's sending all these lovely people and wonderful times. Isn't it glorious, Merry?"

It was. It was wonderful to see the little thin faces from the slums grow round and pink-cheeked. It was marvelous to see the shy little girls and boys gain self-confidence as they learned to swim, row a boat, mow a real lawn, milk a cow and ride a horse. It was more than thrilling to see them sit around campfires and listen to the old, old story and gradually, or all at once, know it was written for each of them.

"I don't like to see them go back," Margaret moaned at the end of one two-week period. "I'd like to keep them here where life is so simple and uncomplicated."

"You'd like to keep the whole world here, wouldn't you, Margaret?" Sam asked as they waved good-bye to the busload.

It was true. No matter how busy she was, Margaret was never busy enough. No matter how many people tugged at her time and heartstrings, she always longed for more and more. Merry looked at her with real envy. *Just once,* she thought, *I'd love to have her energy, her complete selflessness.*

She said as much to Roger one night on the beach when Jou-Jou and her crowd had enlisted them as chaperones.

"Is her selflessness any greater than for a beautiful woman like you to bury herself among people who still live a very primitive life?"

"But it's what I want to do, where I want to be."

"That's the answer."

Two days later Roger called around noontime. "Merry, I've had another call from the city. One of my young patients is seriously ill and I'm going for consultation. I'll fly there at once. Do you have any idea how much I want to stay here with you?"

"I'll miss you, too, Roger."

"Not enough. Will you postpone our date for a few days?"

"Of course I will. And I'll pray for your little patient."

"Pray for the doctors, too, Merry; we need it. And, Merry, you know tomorrow is Keith's birthday. Will you carry on entirely alone? I had thought I'd be of some help. This has been such a big thing building up in his mind. I've promised I'd be there. It's going to be hard to make him understand."

"I know. Why not send him over here before you leave?"

"I'll drop him off if I may and then I can tell you good-bye."

"All right."

It wasn't all right and Merry knew it. It only made things between them more difficult for him to want a special good-bye with her. She knew by the racing of her own heart that she had waited too long here in this pleasant summer place, too long for escape to help her. Roger need not know it, however. She could arrange it so this would be their last good-bye, at least for a long, long time.

It wasn't easy except that Keith kept jumping around them, excited more about the gift his father promised to bring back than he was disappointed over his departure.

The birthday party was a success as far as games, ice cream and hilarity could make it. When it was over and Merry had left Keith in the care of his nurse, she sought again the refuge of the beach and walked for hours on the hard-packed sand.

There was a long-distance call awaiting her when she returned to the house. Of course it was Roger, apparently eager for news of the party and Keith's pleasure in it. "Was it a chore?" he asked.

"No, I loved it. They were just darling, and there was only one fight."

The man roared. "Did you expect more?"

"If you had refereed as many playground altercations as I did this spring, you'd just naturally look for fights when more than two little boys get together."

"I'll have to postpone our date even longer, Merry, and I don't like it a bit. I want to see you tonight." There was deep seriousness in his tone.

"How is your patient?"

"She's very ill, a little girl with polio. There are three of us who stay near all the time. We hope that by massage and constant care she'll escape any serious damage. I won't be able to leave for a week at least. I'll call you tomorrow." He did and each succeeding day as well.

The child's sister and little brother were also showing symptoms, and the doctors were guarding against an epidemic. Roger sounded very tired. Merry stayed on her knees a long time that night; but when she had finished her prayers, she felt there was only one thing for her to do.

In her aunt's room the next morning, Merry talked a while

about a number of things before she announced quietly, "I'm going back tomorrow, Aunt Margaret."

"Oh, darling, no. You have weeks yet before you have to leave. I simply can't spare you."

"I must, Aunt Margaret. There are things I can't seem to do here that I'd like to have ready for the winter's work. I want to have time to orientate Marcia. Think of the surprise she's going to be in that little community and the surprise they'll be to her. Besides, Mr. and Mrs. Murphy write that they can scarcely wait for us to come to see what they've done about their house."

There was no use for Margaret to insist further. The real issue had not been mentioned, nor would it be now. She felt she had no right to intrude into this moment of Merry's life.

"I hate to see you leave, child. It has been wonderful to have you this long. But you know what you have to do. If you can, come back for a week this fall. What will Marcia say?"

"Oh, she's having a fine time here, but she's been eager to go for weeks. She's loved being here, you know, Aunt Margaret, but this will be a new adventure for her. Now if Mother were only well—"

"The shock to your mother has been almost too great. Sam had a report about her this morning early and called to tell me her doctors advise constant care and quiet. She listens to music and dances around her room! She becomes agitated if any of her garments are anything but rose-colored. Poor dear seems to think she's forever getting ready for a ball. She is in a constant state of expectancy."

"How long can it last, Aunt Margaret? This horribly real delusion that keeps her a prisoner?"

"I don't know, darling. No medication has helped her yet. She is getting ready for the inauguration that will never be. It is very real to Druscilla. She has almost stopped eating and Sam says her little strength is due mainly to the supplements she is receiving."

"How can she go on like this?"

"She may not need to for long, dear. The next new medicine may make Druscilla well. Most of all, Merry, we must pray."

The afternoon mail brought a letter from Lucy. "We got married, Miss Merry, Bailey and me, and we're doing real good. His younguns are the sweetest. Mrs. Richards said you'd like to know. Now when you come back, I can maybe be in one of your classes for women. I put up beans and corn and tomatoes already, and I want you to taste my berries. I been canning them for pies this winter."

"She's so young and pretty." Merry was almost weeping as she told her aunt. "If I could have been with her more, talked with her, reasoned with her, she might have waited."

"Nonsense, darling. Bailey would have been talking and reasoning at the same time. At least she caught a vision and she'll keep it. Merry, I believe that girl will be one of your greatest helpers."

"Perhaps so. She loves the Lord, and she and Bailey will have a real Christian home. It will be a light in a dark place. You know, Aunt Margaret, I love you and hate to leave you, but I can scarcely wait to get back to 'my people.' "

19

Welcome for Marcia

THE NEXT MORNING the two girls were in the huge station wagon "heading for the hills."

"Packed like a gypsy caravan," Dr. Sam complained as he helped store boxes and bundles in every available space. "Sure you can manage this load?" he growled. "You go slowly. You hear me, Merry? And don't stop fast. Be sure you've plenty of room."

"Yes, Dr. Sam."

"Merry, if it rains, you'd better do the driving. It's not easy to hande a heavy load like this and Marcia is still not too experienced." He turned to the younger girl. "Honey, you're a good driver. You just mustn't overdo and especially on those mountain roads. Sure you have your credit cards and plenty of change?"

"Yes, sir." This from Merry. "Don't worry."

"Good-bye, darlings." Margaret was laughing at the gruff old man, but he didn't know it. "You'll write to me, won't you?"

"Yes, Aunt Margaret. Thank you for a wonderful summer."

"Merry," Dr. Sam began once more, "stop early enough at night so you won't have to go in a strange motel too late."

"We will, you darling old worrier." Marcia surprised him by leaning out her window and giving him a choking hug. "Promise you'll come up to see us."

"Maybe. I'll be going back to work in a few days and then there won't be time for anything. Not even a trip to the beach," he said regretfully. He stood with Margaret and looked longingly after them. "They are fine girls, Margaret. I'm sorry Merry didn't stay. Did she tell Roger she was leaving?"

"I didn't ask, Sam, but she probably did."

Merry had told Roger, but it wasn't easy because he made it plain he saw no sense in her early departure. "I'll call you at the mission," he stated flatly. "Merry, will you write to me?"

"I'll answer your letters, Roger."

"There's not much chance of saying all one wants on the phone. I'll come up as soon as I can get away." Then he added meekly, "If I may."

"Of course." What else could she have said? Merry wondered later.

※ ※ ※

The closer they came to the mission, the more excited Marcia became. The sight of the first tiny log cabin partially hidden in a distant valley put her on the edge of the seat in amazement. "I've seen pictures of them, Merry, but I never believed they really existed outside of movies. How do you get to one of those places? Do people actually live there? What do they do?"

"That cabin is real, as well as dozens of others you'll see. The people do a little mining, a little gardening and even sometimes a little 'moonshinin'.' "

"Aren't you afraid? Do they carry guns—shotguns?"

"Yes to the guns, but why should I be afraid? They know I'm their friend. Their guns aren't for me."

"Do you have to be careful when you get close to the cabins, like they write about in novels? Do they really go gunning for strangers? Have you seen a feud?" Marcia's questions tumbled after each other so fast Merry laughed until she had to brush the tears away.

"You wait and see. I've lived here for months and I've not seen a feud nor have I seen a person shot. We've treated only two shotgun wounds. One was a man who slipped and almost took his own foot off because his gun went off accidentally; the other was a great hound dog that someone mistook for a deer. I'm afraid we are much tamer than you suspect. Disappointed?"

"Nope. I'm just not going to believe you." Marcia giggled with a teasing lightness she had not had since the tragedy of her father's death. "I'm going to expect mountain lions, mountain dew, feuding, all-night coon hunts, and—and lots of things."

"You'll hear the coon hunts and maybe get invited to go on one as I did. Oh, Marcia, it's just wonderful having you here with me."

It was wonderful, too, to drive up and be greeted by Murphy and Mrs. Murphy. The old couple had only seconds to wonder how to greet the two girls when they were smothered by young arms and kisses.

"I always wanted to hug you and hug you and hug you, Mrs. Murphy," Marcia bubbled, "but I never quite dared. You know, I thought you should have been one of my grandmothers."

"And so I shall be. So I shall be." The old lady beamed and tightened her arm around Merry.

They were laughing with just a hint of mist in their eyes when the mission family came out to greet the travelers.

"It's a good thing you finally arrived," Mr. Richards joked as he led them inside. "Mr. and Mrs. Murphy haven't gotten a thing done today for looking."

"They've always been like our own," the old man said. "Now they know it. Miss Merry, dear, please hurry and come with me. I want you to see our home."

"Indeed and she'll not budge from *this* house until tomorrow." Mrs. Murphy sounded almost militant. "The darlings will rest, they will, before you give them hammer and nails." But they couldn't wait another day. Both girls trooped across the road to Mr. Murphy's plot of ground to admire the good beginning of his first house.

Early that night when they were in their own room, Marcia said, "It's the strangest thing, Merry. I feel as if I belong already. When the men working for Mr. Murphy stopped hammering to shake hands with you and meet me, they acted as if they loved us both, as if we were somehow one of them. I never saw more gentle and kind people. And the two women who are helping in the mission kitchen treated me as if I were their own child. I wonder why you thought it would take time for me to feel at home here."

"Someday the carpenters will tell you their own stories. One spent fifteen years in the state penitentiary. The other dodged the law so long, he still looks startled when the sheriff comes for a visit. They were really old men when they found the Lord and listened to His voice. Now they can't work fast enough, as they say, to make up for all the time they lost. The women are among the sweetest I've ever known. Bandy can't read or write but can quote more Scripture than I with all my work in Bible school. Lizzie is just helping out here this summer. She'll go back to college in the fall to work on her master's degree. Then she'll come back home to be a respected home demonstration agent. Her people love her for what she's planning for them."

"They are all wonderful," Marcia began. "I'm so—"

There was a shout, a blast of gunfire and more shouting that seemed to come from all around the main cabin.

Marcia swished off the light and crept to the window to look out stealthily from behind the blinds. "Wow! What was I saying? What kind of place is this? Are we having an Indian raid?"

Merry practically collapsed on the bed, almost helpless with laughter. "No—no Indians. Just welcome home. I should have thought of this. Come on."

"Welcome? Well, if you say so. But it sounds more as if they want to drive us away."

Mrs. Richards was at the door. "Come on, girls. I know you are exhausted, but the community has turned out. I begged them to wait until tomorrow."

They might have been exhausted, but Merry and Marcia forgot about themselves as they were surrounded by those happy hill people with their jars of jellies and jams, their little baskets of eggs and slabs of bacon, fresh corn from the fields, an apron for each of them made from flour sacks with gay designs and sewn with delicate cross-stitching in bright floss.

Later Merry wrote to her aunt, "I began to wonder whether I was the old timer—or Marcia. Aunt Margaret, she's having the best time of anyone I ever saw. Just think, a few months ago she was nothing but a hothouse flower. Her maturity surprises me. She's not even having trouble understanding people as I did, and the children follow her around as if she were a fairy princess. She acts like it too. Do plan to come up and spend some time with us when things are running smoothly in your work back in town."

She did not include anything in that letter about Roger. It was difficult enough to answer his letters, to wait for his phone calls, and to try to quiet the tumult in her own heart. Roger's calls came almost daily and were apparently none too satisfactory. At last one day he asked, "Can't you talk freely, Merry? Are there always people with you?"

"Yes, usually. Unless I'm in the office."

"When are you there?"

"I'm never sure, Roger. Generally at a time you'd be making hospital calls or operating."

"I won't have it this way, Merry. Why did you go back

so soon?" He had asked her before, and she had hedged as she did now. The surprise came the next night when the phone rang and Mr. Richards answered it. They were all in the dining room finishing a late supper, delayed because of an accident at the nearby mill which had taken them off with first-aid kits and prayers.

The director of the mission turned from the phone with a startled look disappearing from his eyes to be followed by ill-concealed mirth. "A long-distance phone call for Miss Merry Johnson to be taken only in the office."

Merry fled there and closed the door quickly behind her. "Oh, Roger," she gasped when she picked up the receiver, "they'll never let me forget this."

"I guess they won't. This is the way I'll be calling you from now on." He did; it was as if he could talk more freely when he knew Merry was alone.

She couldn't tell him not to call. She didn't want to, nor did she like the feeling that she was so dependent on those few minutes alone each night.

* * *

By the first of December Mr. and Mrs. Murphy had moved into their new home, the school work was going well, the clinic was drawing more and more people to the mission, the church services were growing slowly but satisfactorily, and Roger had made eight quick trips to spend a few hours with Merry.

She tried to divert him from the serious words he had to say. She attempted to find the right answer to the call of his heart, but he brushed aside all her inadequate attempts. "I'll keep coming until you see things my way, Merry," he insisted as they stood high on a trail and looked into the valley below. "I love you so much, Merry, I don't want to wait. I've no patience." He smiled at her and took her hand. "Why can't you love me? Oh, I know I'm no prize, but it seems I love you so much you would have to love me some."

The question remained unanswered. And when they reached the foot of the hill, Roger wasn't sure how she had evaded it again. He knew she had been utterly sweet, but her reply was light, and somehow he felt as defenseless as a callow youth before her sudden sophistication. She had stopped writing to him. She did not encourage his visits, but she could not ask him not to come. There were times she resolved to, but she could not bring herself to do it.

In his plane on the way back to the city, the doctor was aware of only one impression. She liked him very much or she would have been more remote, and she would have insisted that he not call again. Perhaps it was that Merry felt completely dedicated and wedded to her work there. A girl such as she would not easily give up that which she knew to be a call. Roger had assured her he would never stand in her way of Christian service. In fact, he had insisted he would do his utmost to see that she had every opportunity to continue this same kind of work in the city and that they could go to her hills for special days or weeks of work. Could that be it? He pondered and prayed but found no answer other than the conviction that they belonged together and would be together someday for their own happiness and God's glory. How to convince Merry of that was his big problem.

Then he thought of Keith. He could not be what made Merry hesitate, because she obviously loved the little boy.

He would give her more time. Perhaps the months he would be away on the continents of Europe, Asia and Africa for his mission board might teach her what his presence and calls had not. She might find out that she could not be happy without his visits, his calls. Conceit? He smiled at his own audacity. He had seen her eyes in an off-guard moment.

It had happened the week before, when he had brought Keith with him. For once Merry's Saturday was completely free and the weather had suddenly changed to a warmth unnatural to December. They had climbed long trails and stopped at several cabins to be greeted with warm, friendly interest.

"Have you decided he's your man, Miss Merry?" one old lady had asked.

She received the reply "He's a good friend."

"Looks like more than a friend to me for a doctor man to come so far and so many times."

"That's what I've been trying to tell her, Mrs. Miller, but she won't pay any attention to me," Roger said.

"'Pears like she better. She's not getting any younger. Course we'd not like to lose Miss Merry, doctor, but you could come stay with us, too."

"That's an idea," he agreed.

Later as they sat on a rocky ledge and had their lunch, he teased her with words that were more serious than his tone. "I like your Mrs. Miller. She's a woman of great discernment. In fact, I'm going back to talk with her. She knows you are getting to be an old maid, Merry. You'd better marry me fast or you'll lose all your chances."

Merry reached for a ham sandwich. She smiled at the picnic spread before them but did not look at the man beside her. "I'll not take you to see any more of my people, Roger. You give them notions."

"Wish I could give *you* some."

Later that night when they sat in Mrs. Murphy's parlor, Roger, who was leafing through a medical book he had brought for use at the clinic, was really watching Merry.

There were two mirrors in Mrs. Murphy's best room; one caught Merry's reflection. She knew it did, but she did not know that Roger could see in the other mirror her every move reflected from the one she almost faced. And there, in those few moments while he was apparently scanning the book with occasional glances at the fire, Merry looked at the sleeping child in her arms, and the love in her eyes was unveiled.

Roger saw it and his heart rejoiced. Yet she lowered her head and seemed not to hear the last words when he glanced at her with the calm remark "I think it's as good a book for home use as we could find. Merry, let's put it in our own home."

"Why not explain it to Mr. Richards, Roger? There were several things he wanted especially to discuss with you this weekend, and you've scarcely been near the dear man."

"Strange as it may seem to you, Merry, I didn't come here to be near the dear man."

It was then that Mrs. Murphy came in to carry Keith off to bed, and Merry suggested they go over to the recreational hall so she could play for the young people as she often did on Saturday nights.

"Can't anyone else play for them?" Roger growled as he held her coat.

So the conflict in his own heart was great as he flew toward the city. Had he but known the turmoil he left behind, the man would probably have turned his plane and settled the business at once, his patients, operations and office hours forgotten.

As Merry paced around the mission grounds far into the night, she could come to only one conclusion. For her own peace of mind, she must not see Roger for a long, long time. There came flashing across her mind the thought that had been there before. It was a persistent thought which she dismissed as rapidly as it came. Roger was a very understanding person—this she had seen—this she knew. Perhaps he would be totally sympathetic if he knew—but, no. She could not risk the opposite reaction of a man who had wanted a child so badly he had taken an unknown baby to fill the empty place. She could never risk facing the contempt and disgust he might feel. Merry prayed there in the cold winter night and leaned her head against the rough bark of a tall pine. Then she went inside to sleep quickly and dreamlessly for the first time in months. Yet, when she awakened, the girl whose high resolves the night before had seemed so strong knew she was in for a real inner struggle because almost her first thought was *Tonight Roger will call.*

20

December Wedding

MARGARET WAS SICK. Merry had the letter early one morning just as she was watching the children file into the assem-
bly room. She opened it even as she walked toward her seat,
for many times there were little messages to the girls and
boys from "Miss Margaret."

The typewritten envelope gave no indication of the news
inside. "She's really sick, Miss Merry." Becky had found her
way to the typewriter and tapped out the message. It had
been a hard task for her, as the many mistakes indicated, but
she had accomplished her mission. "She doesn't know we
know it, but Miss Margaret is in real pain. I asked the doctor
on his way out, waylaid him in the garden I did. He looked
at me funny-like, then he said, 'Becky, it might be well if she
had her favorite niece with her.' Reckon you ought to bring
Dr. Sam with you, too, Miss Merry?"

While she was trying to get Dr. Sam on the phone and
Mrs. Richards packed for her, Merry promised to send for
Marcia at the best time. "She'd only worry, darling, if she
knew you were missing your school. She'll know I'm ex-
pendable, and Mrs. Richards will take good care of you."

Dr. Sam met Merry at the airport in the city. "I would
have gone on ahead, child, if I had been able to get away.
But I had surgery up to half an hour ago. This may be why

174

she wouldn't come into town this fall. Every time I called out there or went down for a weekend, Margaret would say, 'I know I should hurry back to the clinic, Sam, but there are so many things to see to here at the beach, I can't tear myself away.' She looked pale but she was so all-fired enthusiastic about the new cottages she's having built and the few people who were still staying on in the little houses near the road, I thought she was just enjoying a rest after the busy summer. I should have known better. This is the first time she's ever stayed away past the opening of school. That was her big day in the clinic, with the children coming in to see her and to be encouraged and directed to the community center, to talk over their summer activities, their time at the seaside, and have a treat before they left. She'd urge them to be sure to go to Sunday school and the church services she thinks are so important. What has it all meant to her, Merry? Now she's sick and she won't get any help out of any of it."

"You don't really mean that, Dr. Sam. You couldn't. Every effort on Aunt Margaret's part has been for one purpose—to help people she loves so much to know Jesus as Saviour. You wonder what good it does her even now when she is sick? All the good there is in the world and heaven too. She's responsible for many knowing God the Father, Jesus the Saviour, and the Holy Spirit, the Comforter."

"Yes," he said slowly as if he were thinking out a new problem. "That has always been the important thing to her. And now? Oh, Merry, I'd give my life if I could make her well." His voice broke.

"Would you really, Dr. Sam?"

"Would I? I'd not hesitate a moment. I have loved her from the first day I saw her standing in her yard, a tiny girl even at fifteen, and beautiful beyond belief. There's nothing I'd not do for Margaret. I can't let her die."

"And she won't have surgery?"

"No. I called Dr. Manti as soon as you called me. He said there is a good possibility her cancer can be removed or arrested if she'll only let him try. I didn't even know it, but she was in to see him last week and he's been twice to the beach to see her. He was her father's friend. Merry, why won't she?"

"You'll try to change her mind? You'll try to persuade her to let the doctor operate to save her life?"

"Merry, what a question! Why do you think we're rushing to the seashore?"

"Don't you see, Doctor dear, that's what Aunt Margaret has tried for years to show you? She has wanted you to see that Jesus loved you so much He gave His life for you. Won't you let the burden of sin be lifted from your life just as you want the surgeon to lift the cancer from Aunt Margaret's body? The Lord Jesus didn't just *want* to die for you, Dr. Sam. He really did it. He still is waiting for you to see He gave His all for you. The next move is up to you."

He was in a hurry, this gray-haired man at the wheel. He was speeding down a busy highway toward the bedside of the woman he had loved all his life. But now he was so stunned by the sudden impact of Merry's words that he pulled off to the side of the road and muttered, "I never saw it before. I never realized it had to be for me, too."

"But you do now?"

"I do, my child. I know now. And the verses and the sermons I've heard seem to be running through my stubborn old head all at once. Why did He do it for such as I am?"

"Just love, Dr. Sam, and because He sees you as He wants you to be. Isn't God wonderful?"

There they prayed together by the roadside, this old, brilliant man and the young woman to whom the Holy Spirit had given the right words.

The rest of the miles were soon covered and Dr. Sam, with

Merry clinging to his big hand, opened the front door and slipped quietly toward the kitchen.

"We didn't ring the bell," he explained as Merry hugged the cook and was almost smothered by her endearments. "We thought she might be asleep."

"Sleep or not, you're the best medicine Miss Margaret could have. You had better go on up by yourselves. I'm not going to be the one to tell her you are here. She'll not mind once she sees you. Before that, if I tell her, she's liable to tear me apart. I just had to send for you. I just had to."

"Of course you did, Becky. You did the right thing," the doctor assured her. "We'll go on up now."

There was no answer to Merry's soft rap at her aunt's door, so she turned the knob quietly and looked inside at Margaret sleeping on her lounge by the sunny window.

Then the invalid's eyes opened, glanced at the two standing in the doorway. She closed her eyes again. The next moment she was wide awake, her hands outstretched.

"Merry! Sam! I'm so glad to see you, my dears, but who told you to come! Not Dr. Manti?"

"No." Merry bent to kiss her aunt.

Sam knelt by the couch, both of her hands in his. "Oh, my very dear, why didn't you let me know?"

"I only knew myself a little bit ago. It simply seemed easier to stay here than to get into the rush of life in town. I shall be better now that you are here. Can you stay, Merry, a few days anyway? Sam, I know *you* can always come at will." Her eyes, tired and full of pain, were laughing into his. She, better than many others, knew his dedication to his work and the few hours he took for his own unless he could leave his office well staffed.

"We're here and we're going to stay," he told her with a voice none too steady. "I'll never leave you again, Margaret."

"I'll be back." Merry started for the door.

"No, wait, child." Dr. Sam held one hand toward her;

then he turned to the pale woman on the couch. "Once long ago, darling, you promised that when I accepted Christ as my Saviour, you would become my wife—that very day if I still wanted you." There were tears in the eyes of this gruff man whose hands were gently holding hers.

"You mean, Sam, you've really found the Lord?"

"Merry showed me today."

"He was ready to listen today, Aunt Margaret. I showed him nothing new."

"Of course she didn't. But, Margaret, I've shut Him out so long."

"I know, Sam dear, but now you have the rest of your life to live for our lovely Lord."

"We'll be married this afternoon. I shall carry you down to your living room and Dr. Manti will give you away. I called him while I was at the airport waiting for Merry and he promised to meet me here at four o'clock. We'll have a surprise for him. Merry, you arrange with Dr. Silver. Special license and all that." He spoke as authoritatively as when he had orders for a new patient.

"Sam! Not now!" Margaret's voice was scarcely audible. "Didn't you understand?"

"Understand? That you are very ill? That Dr. Manti has given you only a few months unless you submit to surgery, and you won't do that? Understand that you want to stay here in your pink and lavender room and let the rest of us go on our thoughtless way without paying the least attention to your pain? Of course I understand." He paused and the pause was dramatic. "However, the condition has been met. I know your Saviour as mine, and I want you for my wife more than I ever did."

They weren't aware that Merry had left the room to hurry downstairs to talk and plan with Becky and Horace.

It all worked out as Dr. Sam had said. They *were* married in Margaret's living room in the late December afternoon.

Becky's wedding feast was as elaborate as if she had prepared it for days. "That's because Horace and I worked every minute from the time you came down those steps, Miss Merry, and the cooks that are here on the beach have been coming in and out of my kitchen with everything they could find. We did have a good reception, didn't we?"

Two days later Dr. Sam had his wife enthroned in a hospital room where private nurses came and went at her every sigh.

Merry seemed always to be near her although she did follow Margaret's instructions of closing her apartment and having Becky and Horace pack everything to be moved into Dr. Sam's old stone house.

"Imagine, sweet niece," she said softly after a long day of tests, "all my life I've dreamed of the time I could make a home for Sam. You know, I'm not even fretting that I can't be in on the actual confusion of the move. Somehow I've faith we are going to have a little time together here as well as in the hereafter. Did you ever see anyone as happy as Sam?"

A few days later, under heavy sedation, and ready for the trip to surgery, Margaret held her hand and whispered, "Bend down, darling."

"Yes, Aunt Margaret?"

"Where's Roger?"

"He's in New York planning his trip with his mission board. He'll be back next week."

"Don't keep him waiting, Merry. There's no need."

No need. Merry said the words over and over to herself as she stood by the window of Margaret's room during the hours her aunt was in surgery. She thought of them later, after she had seen her aunt settled once again in her bed with two nurses and Dr. Sam beside her.

"She's going to be all right, Merry," he said over and over.

"I've never seen prettier work than Dr. Manti did. That man is the greatest. She's going to be all right."

It did seem so for the next few days, and then, in the middle of a cold night with snow foreshadowing a more bitter winter, Merry answered the phone by her bed to hear terse words quickly spoken. "I'm calling for Dr. Sam, Miss Johnson. He wants you to come at once. Mrs. Hallack is worse. He told me to call a cab for you. He said the storm is too bad for you to try to drive."

Thus it began, with Margaret sinking in and out of consciousness, apparently free of pain, untroubled about herself but anxious because Sam and Merry were always there and looking tired.

"It's her heart," Dr. Manti told them. "If we can get her through the next two weeks, she'll be all right."

Finally there came the day when he said, "She's out of danger. She'll be out of here soon and as good as new. Now, Sam, get out of here, completely out of this hospital and don't let me see you mooning around this room for another eight hours at least. Don't you have a home where you can go and get some sleep?"

"I'll take a turn in the resident's room here or some other vacant place," Sam replied with tears of relief pouring down his cheeks and his arm around the man who had stayed by his Margaret so steadily. "I'll sleep a few hours, look in on Margaret, and then think about going to my own office."

"Trouble with him," Dr. Manti muttered good-humoredly to Merry, "is that he gets more attention than any patient in the hospital. It's no surprise to Sam either. If I had my way, I'd bar him at the front door. The old coot has every nurse falling over herself. They think if anything happens to his Margaret, he'll bomb the place."

Hours later Merry said to a weak but refreshed Margaret, "I'm glad to be able to go back to the mission, darling. Doubly glad because I know you are going to be all right. I wouldn't leave if there were the slightest danger of your not being well. I'll come down weekends though if you'll have Marcia and me."

She had seen Roger entirely too often, and Merry knew it. He was visiting Margaret one day when her own doctor came in to look at her chart. "I'm not going to observe professional ethics in this case, Dr. Manti," he said with a twinkle in his eyes. "I've known Mrs. Hallack all my life. I claim a better understanding of her case even if I haven't been called in on it, so I'll drop in to see that she gets proper care."

"That's the trouble with you youngsters just out of internship," Dr. Manti said, winking at Margaret and appearing to be very stern. "Now I'd let you do a little bandaging for me if I were rushed, but other than that I'd just let you stand by to learn a few tricks of the trade."

Margaret was laughing as he left. "I don't know how he puts up with Sam, let alone you, Roger. I'm so impressed with my own importance that I'll probably want to retain a room here for years just to be sure of having people come to see me and show concern about the ounces I gain each day."

* * *

Roger took Merry to dinner and over a candlelit table talked of his trip to New York, the lectures he had heard, and the things he was to do.

"Let's make this trip to the mission fields our honeymoon, Merry. You can get away and Margaret is all right."

She took a few seconds to form her answer; and as she spoke, it was as if her hands moved to pick up her purse, her coat and her life that she might handle them alone. "I'm sorry, Roger. I should not see you anymore. I should not have come tonight. I—no, I must go back home. I'll be leaving almost at once."

"But why, Merry? Why? Don't you—"

It was inevitable that so many of their times together had been interrupted by the same old call. Now it was a quiet waiter who stood beside Dr. Blackstone with the message. "It's an emergency, doctor. The hospital asked that you come as quickly as possible."

21

Sand Castle

THERE WERE NO MORE PHONE CALLS when Merry was back
on her mountaintop teaching history and Bible in the school,
visiting among the women, planning the summer camping
program and helping Mrs. Murphy in her little kitchen.
There were no phone calls but letters came daily, letters with
stamps from well-known cities and little villages that were
not even dots on the map. Some she answered, but most she
left untouched after the first eager reading—as if the very
apparent indifference would still the longing within her.

Classes were decimated by measles in April, and the school
was put on half-day sessions so the staff could visit the sick
and help the frantic mothers. Merry and Mrs. Richards went
about until they were almost too tired to stand.

"We might as well try to immunize China as these people
unless we can do something to get them to come to the hospital," Mr. Richards stormed at dinner one night. "They've
lost more children from measles than any other disease that
ever struck here; and from all accounts, this epidemic is the
worst. Do you know what I found this morning? That Car-
son family on Upper Creek had two in bed with high fevers,
and the big boy was out chopping wood with spots still
showing. I wonder now if his mother knew what I was rav-
ing about. She had him inside and on a cot almost as soon as

I started shouting at her, and she looked as if I had struck her. It was only then I realized I had been so incensed." He looked around at his mission family, amazement written all over his usually calm face. "I didn't know I could so far lose my temper."

They were still laughing as they began to discuss plans of helping those so badly affected. "We'll have to call in help from the city if we get any more pneumonia cases. Unless we can get across the idea that the aftereffects can be serious, we'll need more than a little help, too."

The next day on mule and foot, Mr. Murphy and the older boys and girls set out to cover as many cabins as possible to send back those who needed extra care and to impress on the mothers the proper precautions to take for those who were almost well.

"It's a thankless job we've had this day," Mr. Murphy said later to Merry and his wife as he sat with his tired feet propped near the oven door and a steaming cup of tea warming his hands. "The first time I've had a woman take a broom to me, it is."

"And what did you do, my love?" Mrs. Murphy asked.

"Do? I said, 'Strike me if you wish, my friend, but put your big girl by the fire and keep her there with her bare feet out of this cold for another week at least so that I don't have to be digging a grave for the lassie.'

"She lowered her broom and asked, 'Why didn't you say so plainly, Mr. Murphy? My boy says you know better how to plant corn than any of the men on the hill. It's not doctorin' you've taken up, too, is it?'

"Then I told her how books say some things even simple souls like myself can learn and use to help others. She asked me in for coffee and I drank it."

It wasn't all bad and in a few weeks they knew that their labors in their "Samaria" during the epidemic had brought the people closer together. They saw that those who followed the mission nurse and her emergency crew had no deaths in their families and only slightly serious aftereffects. It had never been so before.

"I've heard of such tales," Marcia wrote to her aunt and uncle, "but now I've seen it and heard it. I was in Merry's classroom helping her arrange a display table before class when in stalked one of the most furious women I ever beheld. 'It's all good you did us when we had the measles, Miss Merry, and we're beholden to you for it; but this here boy o' mine got his whoopin' cough right here and he's comin' on to school while he's got it. I don't want him missin' his lessons. He's done too good so far.'

"There was no reasoning with her. Finally Merry said so softly it was almost a whisper, 'The state police won't let us keep a child in school who has a contagious disease.'

" 'You mean they'd come here a meddlin' with you, Miss?'

" 'Yes. They'd come to the school and—'

" 'Come on, Rufe.' She took the boy's hand. 'It's all right to cut up a little, but we're not goin' to let them policemen come here tellin' our teacher what to do. How soon can I send him back, Miss Merry?'

"She left supplied with books for the boy to read, and Merry sagged against the desk. 'I love loyalty,' she sighed.

"This has been a good year. I've loved being here at the mission and going down the trail each morning in the old bus to the little high school. I've studied harder and learned more than ever before in my life. I'm not sure, but right now I think this is the place where I want to spend the rest of my life. Merry teases me and insists Mr. Richard's son may have something to do with that decision. I like Bob, but I know I'm too young to decide anything like that right now. I really mean it, Aunt Margaret. Only think, last year I didn't think I was too young for anything. I'll be eager to come back next fall, but at this moment I can scarcely wait for school to be over so I can run on the beach, wear out your sailboat, eat Becky's surprises, and swim. Most of all I want to talk and talk with you and that blessed uncle you gave us. I may come before Merry does because she has some strange idea of spending most of the summer here."

"Of course we know why, Sam," Margaret said on reading it aloud to him. "What are we going to do about that girl?"

"That's your department, my dear. I can mend broken bodies. I'm not sure of broken spirits. And for all of Merry's bravado, she has heart trouble this doctor can't help."

However, Merry showed no signs of being heartsick when she arrived in mid-June after Marcia had had two glorious weeks of bringing the old place back to life.

"I can only stay a few days," she told her aunt. "I'm going to act as camp counselor."

"Oh, no, Merry. I've counted on you staying here to help with the little girls who will be coming next week."

"You are a darling, Aunt Margaret, and I'm not ungrateful, truly. I've arranged for my roommate at the institute to come and help you if you want her. I must go back. In fact, I feel a bit guilty for taking this much of a holiday."

There was no changing the girl's mind. Margaret told her husband so as they stood on their balcony and looked at the harbor lights.

"When is Roger due back?" she asked.

"Sometime this week. I've had a letter or two from him. The boy has had a good mission, you know, Margaret. I hope he doesn't feel restless as a result of it. He's a good man to have on a mission board, but I'd hate to see him truck off to the uncivilized wilds; I believe he can do more good stirring people up here at home. Hey, see what just went on?"

"You mean—Sam! Lights upstairs in his house!"

"That's what I prayed would happen. I knew he would head to the beach as soon as he got back, expecting Merry to spend the summer here. Just suppose he had been a week later and she stuck to her stubborn notion of leaving us."

"Suppose she won't listen!"

"She'll listen if I have to do a John Alden myself."

Merry had stayed late in the library to read. She had found no rest this week in her aunt's house. She had hoped to have a few hours with Keith, but the little boy was in town with his nurse waiting to come when Roger did.

I shouldn't have come, Merry kept thinking, and wishing she were anywhere else.

Now she turned the pages of a travel magazine without seeing most of the pictures. The magazine was dull even with its bright colors and alluring ads. Neither was the soft music coming from the stereo set at all what she wanted it to be. There was a restlessness within her that sent Merry to her aunt's big desk and the Bible that always lay on top.

She was reading through Psalms when the knock came at the French doors and she turned to see Roger there smiling at her.

"I knew you would be here," he said when he was inside, her hands in his. "Merry, Merry, how I've missed you!"

"I'll call Aunt Margaret and Dr. Sam. They'll want to hear about your trip too, Roger."

"Darling, when will you ever learn that I don't want to see anyone but you? Not even your aunt and uncle! Now tell me about you—and the last few months. Do you know how very unsatisfactory letters can be?"

"No, Roger. Yours were—"

"Just what I meant. Every word of them. And what did I get in return?" He laughed at her confusion and began to talk of India, South America, Hong Kong. "At the rate the calls have come since we landed, I'll have to give up the practice of medicine to go around on a lecture tour. Seriously, I wish all of our doctors could have the opportunity of seeing the world's physical needs firsthand as I have. There would be a lot less complacency. If they could even begin to sense the spiritual needs, we would have a real revival in our midst and real support for our missionaries. Now, Merry, enough of world travels. Tell me. You know I loved you when I went away. That love hasn't lessened; it has grown and grown until I have no patience left for waiting. Has absence taught you what my words didn't?"

She looked down at her hands held so firmly in his and drew them away. "Nothing has changed, Roger. Nothing at all. We'll be far better off if you will accept the—the place of a very good friend. I'm going back home in a few days." She looked up at him quickly then back at her hands folded now so carefully in her lap. "Let's not be serious, not now." Had he misunderstood the eagerness in her eyes when she first saw him at the window? All the encouragement she had given him had been in completely off-guard moments, but each time he had gotten fresh hope, assured that time was all he needed. Now he wondered.

"Not now, Merry? I wonder when you'll stop saying that 'not now'. You know—you must know I can't be your very good friend." They had sat there a long time in the lamp-light with a heavy silence between them, when Roger said calmly, "Keith had planned on a day at the beach with both of us tomorrow. I told him you would probably be here. I'm going to change my own plans and try to meet an old friend in town. Once you took over and threw a birthday party for Keith. How about a twosome beach party?"

In a few minutes he left, and Merry went to her room to begin packing. "I can't wait a week now," she said half aloud. "I'll be ready to go day after tomorrow, but first I must have a glorious day with Keith."

Running away? Yes. It was running again, but it was the best she could do. After she knelt in prayer that night, Merry sat a long time at her window, thankful that Dr. Sam and her aunt had gone early to their room. Suddenly she was overcome by great weariness and stood to look out into the balmy night at the soft summer moon. *I shouldn't be fighting like this. I shouldn't have this turmoil within my heart.* Then she thought of many things and prayed again and once more made a decision. She could never go to Roger with anything but complete honesty between them, nor could she tell him the truth. She could not tell him anything to make him despise her. No, it would be far better to leave quickly and never see him again. He must forget her. She would write one more letter to tell him so. She would tell Dr. Sam he must persuade Roger to—to leave her alone. But would Dr. Sam do it? Not likely. Perhaps Aunt Margaret would realize that what she had tried to do for her niece out of love and kindness was not kindness after all.

* * *

They had picnicked on the beach and the day had been more than perfect. *The Lord has given me a treasure and a setting to remember it in,* Merry thought as she watched the child play on the sand.

"Come, Keith. Before we go back, sit beside me here in the shade and we'll build a castle together."

"We'll build a castle we can live in, Miss Merry. A room for you and a room for me and a room for Daddy and one for Mandy, too."

Merry turned the sob in her throat into a chuckle. "Shall we have a tall house or a long house?"

"We'll have it long and we'll put a tower on it too. I want a tower, Miss Merry, to look out over the sea. I'll have a telescope. You'll get a telescope for me, won't you, so I can see the pirate ships before they shoot at us?"

"A telescope? Of course, Keith, and we'll make a flag all our own to fly above our harbor."

"Miss Merry—" He paused with his little hands full of sand. "Please don't leave me. Please stay here. You can tell me all the things you want to tell your little children in the hills, and I'll listen and I'll remember just like you said you want them to. Please, Miss Merry, stay here."

"Oh, Keith, I love you so very, very much!" She gathered him in her arms for only a moment. "You see, dear, you have a daddy to tell you so many wonderful things. And the little children where I live don't have enough people who can teach them about Jesus and tell them stories. I think He wants me to go back to them. And when you are here in the summer for holidays, sometimes I'll come back and we'll build castles in the sand."

It was then she saw the shadow of the man who had just for a few moments stood near them. "Roger," her voice was almost steady, "I hope we haven't stayed out too long. Keith and I have almost forgotten the time."

"Run along, son. You may play in the water a bit before we go into the house." Roger scarcely waited for the child to leave them before he demanded half angrily, "Why don't you stay?"

"I can't, Roger."

"I want you to. More than Keith does, and he wants you very much. I love you, Merry."

"There's Keith."

"Of course there's Keith. I wouldn't have dared see you often if you hadn't shown an interest in Keith. My wife would have to love him as her own. You must know I've loved you from the first, Merry. I've told you often enough. I thought at times it wasn't fair to rush you; but you wouldn't be rushed, Merry. But now—" He held her hands tightly in his as he talked—almost as if he were sure her answer would be the one he wanted.

"You don't understand, Roger."

"What, darling? You do love me, Merry, or you wouldn't have given me as much of your time as you have. I know that. And you *have* given me your time. And your love?"

"Yes. I've given you my love." But the words held no joy, only misery. She placed her hands against his chest, but the tears on her cheeks and the tone of her voice were more arresting than the gesture. "I didn't intend to," she murmured. "I didn't intend to, but I didn't try very hard not to love you. At first I thought you'd not take me too seriously probably, and no one would be hurt. I thought—"

The man laughed and there was real joy in his heart, for at last he had his answer. "You silly love." He held her in his arms now with his lips against her hair. "You don't have to give up anything to have Keith and me as part of your life, if that's what's making you so miserable. You've given me a vision, too, Merry. Yesterday while I was on my way here, I thought a long while about what your Mrs. Miller said. Today I was with our home missions secretary asking if I might share your mountain top—if you'll have me. Don't look so surprised, Merry. He's an old friend of mine. My work now is interesting, but I want to give everything. They need another doctor in your area and need him badly. We could build a hospital." He was smiling into her upturned face. "Now, darling? Will you say yes now?"

"I can't, Roger!" Suddenly she had to tell him; there was no other way. "Even when we were in grade school, Mike was the very special boy whom I liked best and who liked me." Her words rushed on as if in saying them, she would end forever the conflict between them. "When he went into service, we decided to be married although we knew my parents would—object. We were going to anyway before he went overseas. Mike was killed just before he was to have his last leave—a car accident." Her voice broke. Her hands were gripping the arms that held her, but Merry rushed on tonelessly as if she dared not stop. "When you found me weeping in the garden, it wasn't for my father, but for the little boy I abandoned because my father— But that's not important," Merry sobbed, hurrying her words, unaware of his efforts to draw her closer. "What is important is—I wanted to go away without telling you. I didn't want to tell you of—what happened before I knew the Lord. I wanted to make you stop seeing me without having you despise me. Roger, Keith is my little boy."

She didn't wait to see the shock in his eyes. She couldn't. Merry turned and ran up the path toward the house. She would pick up her bag, say good-bye to her aunt and uncle and Marcia, and be gone before another hour had passed. Like a surgeon's sharp knife, this was probably the better way. Roger would not be interested in sharing her mountain-top now. He would never want to hear of her again and—

But a hand on her arm swung Merry around, and she faced the man she had not expected to see again.

"Isn't that all the more reason you should stay with Keith and me?" he asked as if she had not left him at the water's edge.

"But, Roger, didn't you understand—"

"I understand you are the loveliest person I know, and I love you. I understand now the great reason that makes you want to devote your life to young people. I know why you depend so strongly on the Lord and want to serve Him when you come from a background where He was scorned. I think I know something of the despair and joy you felt when you saw Keith's picture last summer. I love you, Merry. Will you believe that? We will begin a new life together. Shall we take Keith to your land of hills and valleys?"

"Yes, Roger, yes, yes!" The look of longing and love in his eyes, the hunger and demand of his lips on hers melted for-ever the old sorrow of being a woman alone, set apart by her own strong will. In the brief moment she surrendered in his arms, Merry knew the Lord had answered the prayer of her heart, the prayer she had not dared to utter.